# The Resillant

# The Resillant

*Be not overcome of evil, but*
*overcome evil with good.*

*Romans 12:21*

## D. L. Smoot

What was it about her? Kenya Palmer was a hot head, and if it wasn't for the grace of God and strict discipline, she would probably be a world of trouble. Myles Vincent on the other hand, one who was successful, cool, calm and collective, and it would be all those things that fueled and shaped them, that would affect their lives in the end. Kenya and Myles were from close knit families, but it was a childhood tragedy that would rip those families apart for a season. Both coping the tragedy very differently, it was the secret that the cool, calm, Myles was harboring, that would reap the most chaos. Though the Vincent and the Palmer families had long reconciled, Myles harbored a secret hatred for the Palmers and targeted Kenya, sabotaging her in every way that he could think of, but it was her hot headed attitude that would quickly become her stumbling block in most circumstances. As time passed, those obstacles seemed to become more of a stepping stone as Kenya began to mature and overcome all that was thrown her way. Myles became more restless as he watched her career advance, thinking of one more stumbling block that might crush her soaring spirit, figuring public humiliation would be best to break her, since she liked being such a public figure. This time the plan would involve his lover, but when hearts became involved, the game became real, and resulted in a battle that would take the ultimate resiliency to resolve, or as Grandma Rose calls it, "The Resillant".

# Chapter 1

Of the two Palmer girls, Kenya was the youngest, but definitely the most outspoken and self-proclaimed leader. Older sister Olivia was confident enough to go along with her, especially if it meant that Kenya could get them what they wanted with their parents.

The Palmer's backyard, with its patches of missing grass and that wooden fence with openings just large enough for the neighborhood kids to enter when they came over to play or maybe for Olivia and Kenya to see who was coming and going, but regardless of its use, was the favorite gathering place for the neighborhood kids when school was out for the summer, and so it was on this hot summer day. It was beginning to be about lunch time and the kickball crowd had begun to scatter as Olivia stood bouncing the ball as she watched the crowd disperse turned to notice Teddy, the cute pudgy eight year old from down the street, still standing there with a distant smile as he stood there twisting from side to side, hands in his pockets, seemingly mesmerized with Kenya. Maybe he had a thing for mean girls because the meaner she was to him the more he fell for her, however, he was startled out of his daydream as Kenya yelled, "Go home Teddy! Catch up with your brother, he's leaving you!" huffing and placing her hands on her imaginary hips as she watched him make his way through the opening of the fence and run down the street. The neighbor's dog thinking he wanted to play tagged along so he sped up a little more as he now had the dog's full attention, and adjusted his speed accordingly. Olivia watching and laughing, "That kid can run pretty fast to be such a big boy!" she replied as she taunted Kenya about her crush.

The yard was empty now, with the exception of the girl's best friend Chloe, who was between the ages of the Palmer girls. Olivia eleven and Kenya nine so at ten years old Chloe was a perfect fit and like a sister, though Kenya was still considered the boss.

Time, as well as the sun, stood still as they double-dutched and sang. It was Chloe's turn again as they switched up while she backed up to the edge of the yard almost into the flower bushes to get a good running start then hopped right in. The three quickly began to grow bored since the kick ball crowd had dispersed. The humidity had the girls longing for a nice refreshing swim and debating among each other about who should ask for mom's permission to go for a swim at Cantonville Lake which was maybe a couple of blocks behind the Palmer home. There was a favorite spot at the lake with plenty of shade trees where the kids of the neighborhood played but always accompanied by an adult. The trio played a little longer before they decided they'd had enough of the sparsely shaded back yard and were still attempting to work up the courage to go inside to ask Mrs. Palmer if they could go for a swim. "But I didn't bring my swim suit!" exclaimed Chloe. "It's okay you can wear one of mine" Kenya quickly replied before she could finish her sentence, although she knew that they did not wear the same size. "Olivia, you're the oldest you should ask!" Kenya went on. "Oh no, we need someone sweet and innocent," Olivia replied as they both looked at Chloe as she peered back with those big round eyes that seemed to change colors with her mood. "Well I'm not asking alone!" replied Chloe. "Just give her those little puppy dog eyes" Olivia exclaimed as she smiled innocently, fluttering her lashes. However, they decided that it would take all three to handle this task. Feeling a little more confident the three made their way into the kitchen, skipping up to the counter where Mrs. Palmer, known as Sondra by neighborhood friends and family, was standing. She had lunch prepared for the girls and was working on dinner, such pleasant aromas of fried chicken, mashed potatoes and green beans with dinner rolls. Being the third grade teacher at Cantonville Elementary School that meant that she was out for a few weeks in the summer and had a little extra time to prepare those desserts that everyone loved, which happened to be apple pie on today. Sondra was stood at the counter slicing an apple while eating the peelings as she turned to look as they came to a halt not having to wonder long about what they were up to, deciding they would ask all at one time, pushing Chloe up front since they figured it would be less likely that Mom would say no to her. After the girls sang their request, Sondra politely smiled, as she sat their glasses of lemonade and grilled cheese sandwiches on the counter, with a very stern "No." and though she didn't wear glasses, she gave them the over the rim stare that she at times used with her students in the classroom, by this the girls knew it was not a good time to challenge her answer. "You girls know that you are not allowed out there without being accompanied by an adult, and I am not able to leave these chores undone, nor am I able to leave this food cooking on the stove!" How could they respond to such a sweet "no" meaning the lemonade and sandwiches, as they hurriedly finished their refreshments and headed out the back door, Sondra chuckling to herself as she watched them marching in unison out the door and into the backyard, ponytails bouncing and swaying along the way.

Both girls had their Father's height, tall and lanky. Chloe's legs weren't quite as long as the Palmer girls and wasn't near as lanky but she didn't let that stop her from keeping up. Olivia's features were more like their father, Nathan's while Kenya resembled Sondra regardless she was definitely more of a Daddy's girl. Although only two years older Olivia felt that she had outgrown that cute stage since she was heading into the preteen years and preferred being inside now that she was nearly twelve. "But someone has to keep an eye on the little ones" sighing as she would follow them out the door.

The girls had not given up on the notion of the lake so when noticing from the kitchen window that Mrs. Palmer had become distracted by a phone call, decided that they would sneak off to dip their feet in the lake and play at the water's edge for a minute and be back before she realized that they were gone, so through the opening of the fence they went, as they stooped and tiptoed through the grass as if Sondra could actually hear their steps, giggling and running the short distance down the street and to the tree line as they took the short cut, stooping past the bushes pretending to be on a secret mission, as one by one they covered one another while they ducked and dodged through the tree line until they had made it to the other side of the hill way out of view of the Palmer house. Once they were out in the open area, peeking over their shoulders and laughing aloud as they made a mad dash towards the lake. Having so much fun as they rolled up their pant legs and hiked up their shorts while playing in the soothing shallow waters. Those few minutes seemed to fly by and before they knew it nearly twenty minutes had come and gone. Knowing they needed to head back home Olivia and Kenya began to bicker as normal, this time about what they should say if Sondra discovered that they had been gone when they noticed that Chloe had disappeared and the splashing of water that they were hearing was no longer the sound of her playing in the water but rather of her desperately trying to stay afloat. They were in a more secluded area of the lake where there was no by passers, so it had gone un-noticed by anyone that Chloe had started to wander off drifting out into deeper water and was in a panic. Olivia yelled to Kenya to go get help as she ran into the waters and dove in. Kenya began to hesitate when she realized the trouble that they would be in but ran as fast as her legs would carry her when she saw the desperation of her friend. The swimming lessons that the Palmer's enrolled the girls in were paying off as Olivia swam towards Chloe. Chloe franticly fought as Olivia reached for her. It wasn't until Chloe started to go sink further into the water as Olivia was able to grab onto her to pull her up, and back to shore. By this time Kenya had made it back to the lake with Mrs. Palmer as well as several of the onlookers from the other side of the lake had dialed 911. An exhausted Olivia had made it back to the embankment with Chloe, tired but desperately trying to revive her as she lay unresponsive. Several on lookers were gathering and heading over to assist. Everything seemed to be moving in slow motion without sound as Kenya focused on Mrs. Palmer moving through the small crowd that was approaching and grabbing onto Chloe, desperately pleading for her to come back while she did all she could while conversing with 911 on speaker phone. Chloe's parents Valerie and Paul Vincent along with her brother Myles, whom Sondra had Kenya call from the land line as she was dialing 911 on her cell, were all arriving at the same time as the ambulance. Mrs. Vincent reached for her unconscious daughter with Mr. Vincent speaking to her ensuring her that everything would be alright and holding on to Mrs. Vincent while the paramedics worked to resuscitate Chloe while loading her into the ambulance. Myles reached out to touch her hand and tell her everything would be okay and he would see her at the hospital as the paramedics got her situated in the ambulance with Mrs. Vincent frantically hopping into the ambulance beside Chloe, refusing to leave her side as the ambulance quickly took off for West Memorial Hospital as Mr. Vincent and Myles ran to the car to follow after the ambulance while Mrs. Palmer along with the girls ran home scampering to make sure that she'd turned the stove off as she gathered her purse, and the phone to call Nathan as she and the girls hopped into the car, Olivia wrapped in a warm blanket that she had grabbed while inside as she and Kenya sat there quiet without a word to say as Sondra drove as fast as she could to the hospital to check on Chloe. If she had been followed by a policeman they would have had to follow her on to the emergency room that day. Making it into the hospital, she hurriedly stepped down the hallway toward the emergency room lobby with Olivia and Kenya at her heels as they came upon the Vincent's Val turned looking at Sondra through her tears while shaking her head motioning no. Paul's voice beginning to break as all he could manage was "unable to revive." The families huddled together, Sondra taken aback and breathless, asked through her tears if there is anything she could do while letting them know how sorry she was. Val inconsolable and unable to speak it was Paul who let her know that they would give them a call if they needed anything. The call that the Vincent family would make that day to Chloe's older sister Shannon, who was away at Central State University in Hartmont, AL, would be the hardest call they'd ever have to make.

Sondra and the girls made it home just as Nathan was pulling into the garage, as they entered into the den hugging and at a loss over Chloe, saying a prayer for the Vincent's before the girls headed off to their room, as Sondra had already let him know what had gone on. Nathan gave the Vincent's time to be able to gather themselves, then later that evening walked down the street to the Vincent home to show his love and support for the family, but there was no answer at the door as he knocked and the garage door was closed, neither was there an answer on the phone, figuring maybe they had gone to pick Shannon up from the dorm, he slowly headed home where he peeped in on the girls. Both he and Sondra sat on the bed talking with and consoling the girls until they were drifting off to sleep, however, it was a sleepless night for Sondra and Nathan having their minds on the Vincent's. Sondra waited to hear from her friends so that they could let her know what she could do for them in preparation of the funeral, however days passed and the call never came. She was finally able to reach the Vincent's on Friday evening, as Myles answered and let them know the funeral arrangements and where to send the flowers, which is information she had already gathered from the funeral home and sent flowers on the day before, but was looking for the chance to support them and pay her personal condolences and just to be with them in the time of need. Neither Val nor Paul answered their cell nor was able to come to the house phone but she was able to have a very short conversation with Shannon, as Sondra let her know that she was there for them and she loved them. Sondra with the comforter over her face and back turned to Nathan while they lay there in bed that night unable to sleep, as Nathan pulled Sondra close as he attempted to console her and she snuggled against his chest. She would always feel that guilt of losing Chloe. Without speaking a word they knew they had also lost their best friends and couldn't begin to imagine what the Vincent's were going through, neither would ever want to be put in the position of knowing such a horrible tragedy. In the quiet of the night, they lay hand in hand till eventually the ray of the sun light began beaming through the thickness of the window coverings.

The funeral was on a Saturday at 1:00 o'clock in the afternoon as families and community slowly filled the halls of the Faith Fellowship Baptist Church where Pastor Henry Newcomb, a tall and heavy figure with salt and pepper hair and a stern look stood and greeted the crowd. He had a serious look about him but there was always a smile and lots of laughter hiding behind those glasses and sternness of his demeanor. He was a retired Army Veteran with plenty of stories to tell. Being Pastor for nearly twenty years he had officiated many baptisms, weddings, funerals as well as celebrated many graduates. He'd seen many babies being born into the families with Chloe being one of those. Just a few years earlier the girls had all been baptized together. Charlotte was his wife and First Lady of Faith Fellowship Baptist. Neither was soft spoken and Mrs. Charlotte maybe due to her background as a retired Social Worker or maybe due to the three sons and daughter that she and Pastor Newcomb had together, but she always had a word of advice, and her advice on this day would seem exceptionally challenging for the Vincent's, however much needed as they watched the families grow apart in their time of loss. Pastor Newcomb was very supportive as he and first lady ministered to the family grief counseling. They were there for the Palmer's as well. The Palmer's had grown up in that church and community and had introduced the Vincent's to Life Fellowship after they moved into the neighborhood over ten years ago. Loving the bond the church had with the families as well as the community they immediately joined and remained members.

Myles was seated between maternal Grandmother Rose Bellevue, and Shannon who was at times inconsolable, other times in a daze. Myles put his arm around her shoulder as he reminisced of happier times that when they would spend time in the summer with Grandma

Rose in Thibodaux, LA. All the wonderful times they would share and always that big bear hug that made them laugh. Back then he was small enough to lay his head on Grandma Rose big soft shoulders and all would be well, remembering the comforting she was but Grandma Rose had grown feeble and was needing the support of his arms on today. Calm and supportive, he took in everything going on around him throughout the service, all the condolences and every hug being very attentive to all that Pastor Newcomb was saying, that is until his mind began to reminisce about their last conversation. He had put her out of his room and called her nosey. He said that she was just looking for something to tell, and knowing Chloe, that was true, but if he'd had known that this may be his last time seeing her, he would have never let her leave. He wiped his eyes and resisted the urge to give in to those tears so he turned his attention towards the audience of supporters as his gaze tended to linger on the Palmers.

Sondra was very emotional during the service thinking back on how the girls had wondered off from the backyard while in her care. Chloe had spent so much time with her girls that she was like a member of her own family. Nathan, a writer for city paper the Cantonville Herald and well respected member of the community, had been a pillar of support for his family. The Cantonville Community was a close knit one and it was apparent with the growing support of the community with the never ending cards, flowers and food that had been distributed at the Vincent home and church hall, as the gatherers greeted the family, however the Vincent's resisted every effort of the Palmer's toward any comfort or support. As crowd had gathered at the cemetery which was within walking distance of the church grounds, there was a coldness by certain members of the community as well toward the Palmers. The crowd began to file slowly back into the church and into the dining hall. The Palmers didn't stay to eat, though the girls were adamant to stay to be with their friends and did not understand the reason that they were having to leave so soon.

In the weeks to come, Nathan remained very supportive toward his family but could be of little to no support to the Vincent's with their continued avoidance. The Palmer's understood that there would need time under the circumstances, so they agreed to give the Vincent's the time and space that they needed. Not only did they miss Chloe's presence, but the friendship and companionship of the Vincent family as well along with certain members of the community. This was a difficult thing since they had grown so close and had been there for one another since the Vincent's moved into the neighborhood over ten years ago. Attending one another's cook outs and family functions had been a regular thing.

# Chapter 2

The remainder of the summer was a very quiet one for both the Vincent's and at the Palmer's. No longer that same crowd that used to gather in the Palmer's yard to play instead it had grown over, no more missing patches of grass and the gate had been mended. Still only a couple every now and then would come around to enter at the side entrance to play, and even then they could not stay long, so the girls were ready to get back to school as the fall of the year rolled around and school shopping had to be done. They had to have their supplies and book bags and don't forget the new fall wardrobe. The Palmer's weren't rich but they didn't want for anything and Sondra was definitely a Coupon Queen who knew how to stretch a penny. Nathan was just glad that Sondra was taking the girls school shopping this year. That being one trip that he didn't care to go on. As Sondra and the girls headed out for their day of shopping he thought back on some of their previous shopping trips with a nervous laughter as if Sondra might change her mind. Settling back into his recliner in front of the television as they headed out the door while he reflected back on those shopping trips in which he would find himself sitting on a bench outside of the department store as Olivia tried on everything in the store. It was the year before, that's when she claimed to be looking for a distinctive style and wouldn't give up till she found it. Kenya having done her shopping had ended up on that bench beside him attempting to convince him to leave her there while the two of them get dinner. After spending over thirty minutes in the dressing room Olivia emerges and decides that she'd like to go back to the first Department Store, a suggestion that ended with Nathan escorting them out of the mall, but dinner first before heading back home for the shopping trip to resume on the next day with Sondra. "For goodness sakes Olivia, you wear uniforms!" Nathan exclaimed as they were leaving the mall. "Dad, I'd just like for my uniform to fit" she quickly corrected herself "I mean, look a certain way." "What Kenya" Olivia exclaims, as she catches a glimpse of Kenya who was rolling her eyes. "It's not that I don't know what I want, I know exactly what I want, but that department store didn't carry it." Olivia went on to explain. "Really Olivia, I wish you had discovered that two hours ago!" added Kenya. "Daddy and I are starving!" She went on as Nathan distracts the two with the mention of their favorite restaurant, as they pull up and excitedly hop out of the car as if the whole trip was to get to Lowery's Seafood & Grill, and all was well in the world. But that was last year, this year Sondra was careful not to buy them clothes alike, via request big sister Olivia, who now needed her own identity and preferred wearing the skirts now and insisted on carrying a purse, whereas Kenya would wear any pant that she would be comfortable in, and no fancy slippers because she can't run in those, but she did prefer fancy sneakers. Sondra made sure they had all the supplies they needed and everything ready for the semester.

Finally, the first day of school was upon us, a day on which no one had to wake the girls. They were already up getting ready and profiling in the mirror before Sondra could even finish cooking breakfast. She turned the stove off then headed up the stairs, looking in on the girls, yet still surprised that they were dressed. She peered in just as Kenya was pushing Olivia away from the mirror, "You've had enough time in front of that mirror Olivia, you should get tired of looking at yourself!" exclaimed a frustrated Kenya. "That's enough girls, you both look good! Just make sure that you have all the supplies that you'll need for your classes and go on down to eat breakfast before the bus gets here!" Sondra shouted back into the room as she rushed down the hall to finish getting dressed. Although Sondra worked at the school and the bus had such a longer route the girls liked to hang out with their friends is what they told Sondra, truth is they didn't really want to be seen hanging around their mom so they caught the bus to school. The only difference in their uniforms were that Olivia was wearing a skirt and Kenya was wearing khaki shorts. Grabbing their book bags and Olivia making sure she didn't forget her new purse they ran down the stairs to the breakfast table but before they could finish their breakfast they could hear the bus coming down the street, so Kenya with bacon in hand and Olivia stuffing her toast along with the strip of bacon that she had left into her new purse as they yelled goodbye to Sondra ran out the door and was fast enough to be standing there waiting when the bus came to a stop. If only the rest of the days could go as well as this one, thought Sondra to herself as she combed through her hair and watched from the window while they boarded the bus.

Mr. Wagner with his hat sitting high as he sat behind the wheel with the persona of an officer, giving his usual greetings as student's boarded the bus. He was the bus driver for the Elementary and Junior High and as the bus door sprang opened was impressed, but not surprised, since it was the first day of school, at the fact that he didn't have to wait for anyone to come running down the driveway or break up a bickering match while they boarded, so he enjoyed the first week as much as the students since everyone was always raring to go and reserved his energy for later. Kenya took her usual seat about the third row back on the left, scooting her way over her neighbor in the aisle seat to get to her spot near the window. The face that she had grown so accustomed to, had been replaced by an elementary schooler, named Gracie Dalton, a chubby cheeked second grader with freckles and glasses who tried her best to make conversation with Kenya, but of course Kenya's mind was elsewhere as she continued to stare out the window with her mind on the conversations that she'd shared with Chloe during their long bus rides. Olivia sat with the older group towards the back of the bus. As usual they both were excited about the first day of school, however as they arrived they noticed that things seemed to have changed even there.

Arriving in the classrooms there were many stares and whispers, some out of sympathy because they knew they had lost their friend, some were business as usual or I've missed you! Then there were those of resentment, because they'd heard that the Palmer's were at fault for Chloe's death. Both Olivia and Kenya seemed to handle losing their friend as well as to be expected, however, Olivia was much better at handling conflict by avoiding it while Kenya seemed to welcome any challenge. Furthermore, certain things tended to trigger an occasional nightmare for her Kenya. Counseling seemed to help and as time went by, the nightmares were less and less with time, however it seemed that stress would be the thing that would sometimes trigger her nightmare to recur.

That school year Kenya began to write poetry and with Nathan being a writer would naturally feel compelled to read them. He'd slip into her room while they were out in the yard or gone to the grocery store to read her writings, sometimes with a smile and other times he seemed to be concerned. This particular day he looked a little concerned with what he was reading. He left off reading when Sondra called him into the den, but he wondered not so much where her writings were coming from because he knew that answer, but where they would lead. This caused him to pay closer attention to her although he knew he had no need to worry because maybe he didn't say it aloud, but although she was a little head strong, both his girls constantly made him proud.

# Chapter 3

There came a breakthrough that fall between the Vincent and the Palmer family when Val, also a teacher with the Cantonville School System, felt compelled to stop by the Palmer home on her way home after the school's Fall Carnival, an event that Val and Sondra would normally host together. This year everything was very different for them as they had grown apart, and had been passing by one another in the halls without saying a word. Sondra offering a smile, just a way of letting her know that she'd be there whenever she was ready to talk, but Val would look right past her. The girls noticed as well and it made them very sad. Sondra and Nathan prayed together for their friends that with God would help them find the peace and forgiveness they needed. On this particular evening Val pulled up in the driveway of the Palmer's home hesitantly getting out of the car while thinking and practicing in her head about what she would say, knowing that it had been several months since she had spoken a word to her old friend. She paused as she headed toward the door then nearly turned around, taking a deep breath as she looked toward the part of the yard where the kids would play, saying to herself, "Chloe would want me to do this." Straightening her skirt, she gathered enough resolve to approach the door as she headed up the sidewalk and quickly rang the doorbell before giving herself a chance to change her mind. Sondra stood there silent for a moment as she answered. The girls were shocked to see Val standing at the door, not knowing quite what to expect, they stood there silently at the top of the staircase and watched their interactions. It was Val who reached out first to Sondra, then the tears began to flow while they hugged each other as though they had not seen each other in years. The bitterness seemed to dissolve away, Val within this moment realizing how much she had been needing her friends as she looked in to Sondra's tear filled eyes. All Sondra could think about was how God answers prayers as Val expressed her feelings letting Sondra know that she was sorry for blaming her, and knows how much Sondra loved Chloe as well, and did not mean for such an awful thing to happen. Sondra breathed a sigh of relief although she still blamed herself, but just the fact that Val would find it in her heart to forgive her meant so much to Sondra. It meant the world to Val as well to be able to accept and forgive. This was a huge burden being lifted from both their shoulders and as they sat on the couch the girls slowly made their way down stairs to give Val a hug as well. Val thanked Olivia for pulling Chloe out of the lake, and Kenya for going for help and for calling them, and Sondra for attempting to resuscitate and doing all she could to try and save her little girl. By the time Nathan arrived home the living room was filled with ladies and girls crying and hugging. He joined in as well when he saw Val. Val admitted that she would never have peace until she came to a resolution with them, and had been missing their friendship, all the cook outs and family togetherness that they were used to and promised although she realizes it wouldn't be quite the same, there would be other times for the families to come together.

Thanksgiving was a quiet one for both families, but when Christmas rolled around they decided that they would have dinner together at the Palmer's. The Palmer's had gotten up early to exchange gifts and had breakfast as Sondra prepared dinner, before she knew it was 2 o'clock, doorbell rang and all of a sudden the busyness began as the Vincent's filed in and it was almost like the years before. They even brought Grandma Rose with them, wearing her bright red dress looking like Mrs. Clause. Pastor and First Lady Newcomb stopped by as well.

They had pulled names, so they exchanged gifts and enjoyed the wonderful Christmas dinner prepared. Sondra who'd decided to do the traditional this year, which included the turkey, dressing, ham, potato salad and green bean casserole, and it wouldn't be Sondra without baking at least one desert, so she sneaked in their traditional family holiday favorite which was coconut cake. Val decided to do the non-traditional this year and brought the chicken and seafood gumbo and stuffed crab. Being Creole and originally from Louisiana she specialized in the sea food recipes, and she likes them spicy. It seemed that she had been pre-occupying herself with cooking lately. This year even Shannon was included in the holiday cooking so she brought desserts. It wouldn't be Christmas if she didn't do pecan pralines, but cheese cake being a favorite of hers, she had to try more than one flavor, so in the spirit of the season baked cranberry along with pumpkin cheesecake. Olivia and Kenya was in charge of making the holiday punch which Nathan jokingly accused them of spiking. Sondra and Val seemed to have a bit of a competitive edge in the kitchen so dinner was delightfully delicious. It was a healthy and friendly competition and one that spectators definitely enjoyed and benefited from. The husband's had always suggested they consider catering together as a part time business. Gathering in the dining room Pastor Newcomb blessed the food. He and First Lady enjoyed dinner and spending time with the families but wasn't able to stay long afterwards because of their grandkids who were to be arriving later in town that afternoon to spend Christmas evening with them. After dinner Nathan and Paul spent the majority of the time outside after dinner as they normally would, getting caught up on sports and the goings on in the community, especially with Paul being the Cantonville Community College Football Coach. Good way to work off some of the calories from all of the foods eaten also before returning for second rounds.

They couldn't pass by the basketball goal without playing a game of horse. Myles came out just long enough to play the winner before he slipped back inside for seconds. Nathan and Paul settled into the add on to the garage that Nathan called his man cave, with its worn out sofa and recliner chair and makeshift footstools, that were really storage boxes, that also served as tables where they'd placed their plates as they watched the football games because the women and the kids were in charge of the TVs in both the den and living room and this was their man's world, that is until Sondra and Val finds out that there is a good game on and come out to join them, but on today they could enjoy the amenities of their man cave. They had Myles bring food and drinks from the kitchen as they watched their games, while Sondra and Val were catching up on the events and school news among the faculty, in other words, they were gossiping, and Grandma Rose was not shy to let them know that, as they sat at the kitchen table laughing at everything and everybody. Every now and then there was a reflective silence when they glimpsed the kids. Sondra had a way of pulling Val right back into the conversation as they and Grandma Rose sat around the kitchen table. Myles, the only male among the kids, found himself bearing the brunt of the jokes between the girls as they played their game of Twister that Val had bought the girls for Christmas. He didn't mind the attention, however nothing seemed to be as fun without Chloe.

Time went on, and before long Olivia was graduating from college and following in Sondra's footsteps venturing in the career field of education. She had become a Science Teacher at Cantonville High, and Kenya was about to enter her first year of college. The Vincent's had gone on to do well for themselves as well. Shannon still never missed an opportunity to prank Myles or the girls whenever she had the opportunity. By now she was a nurse and had a family of her own, twin sons Randy and Raychard who were seven, and a daughter, Jasmine who was four. Her husband Desmond Richards was a Doctor at West Memorial where they both worked. Myles having grown to be rather controlling and regimented throughout the years, was very successful although he'd had no wife and kids. Paul and Val tended to put a little pressure on him to find that wife so that they could have them more grandkids. Having completed Larson University in Cantonville, and had gone on to be the Regional Manager for the prestigious department store Stroudman and Marcus, with its home base in the Atlanta area, but it was his several real estate deals and ventures that yielded him great success. Money, power and control was something that Myles thrived on, and those things seemed to take precedence over a wife and kids for him. Although miles from home, he loved his family and kept in touch and kept them updated on the happenings in the Atlanta area and would come home when he had the chance and they would visit him in Atlanta. During the summer the family would sometimes travel to Atlanta and stay in some of his rentals properties.

# Chapter 4

Kenya had taken a summer job before her first semester of college at a factory that seemed to be all well from first appearances. It was called Electrotech, where computer part were manufactured and assembled. Proud of having her own money and being able to buy for herself, she opened her first bank account and finally bought her first cell phone. It seemed like she was the only one among her friends who didn't have one and would teased because her friends were still having to call her on the house phone. She was able to purchase one at a discount through Electotech. That discount shopping gene from Sondra was starting to kick in now that she had her own money. Nathan and Sondra were quick to remind her to that she would still need to put back for school supplies as well. One of her co-workers, Jasmine Hinton, was a friend and classmate of Myles took notice of Kenya and decided to give Myles a call. When speaking with him she mentioned to him how she was now working with Kenya Palmer. She had remembered Chloe's drowning and was one who treated Kenya a little cold and aloof. Myles confided in her of how he really felt about the Palmers, only friendly with them for his family's sake but couldn't bring himself to care for them after Chloe's drowning. She mentioned that Kenya seemed a little too uppidy for her, and remembered her to be somewhat of a hothead. She went on to mention that she would love to find a way to get her fired. She gave a couple of the co-workers, with whom had also been close friends with Myles and herself, a call afterwards and gave them a heads up and let them know who Kenya was. Kenya was better at handling those types of ordeals than she used to be so she was able to ignore and avoid the altercations with her co-workers and was just grateful to have a job, however, eventually the stress started to rekindle the nightmares that she'd have from time to time, and this happened to be one of those restless nights. Finally drifting off to sleep the dream began, the same dream every time. She found herself alone at Cantonville Lake. One moment she is on the banks of the lake at night time with a warm wind blowing, then all of a sudden she's under water and as she attempts to swim back up towards the surface she finds herself face to face with Chloe. Uncontrollably she drifts closer and closer to her as Chloe remains motionless except for her hair flowing with the waves of the water with eyes are closed, but as she drifts closer face to face, she suddenly opens them. She is so close that she can see even the color of her eyes as she reaches for Kenya. Chloe is saying something to her, but she can never understand what she is saying. Unable to breathe at this point, Kenya would wake up flailing to get away, gasping for air and covers so wet with perspiration as if she'd literally been underwater, however, relieved that it was only a dream. Grasping around in the dark for the light switch as she changed out of her sweaty sheets and pajamas then able to drift off to sleep to be re-wakened nearly thirty minutes later by the alarm clock. Although she felt like crawling back under the covers that Kenya Palmer determination kicked in and was ready to start her day.

Kenya had been on the job for nearly two months now and had decided to continue working at Electrotech throughout college. With barely 4 hours of rest Kenya started her work day. A little more tired than usual after having one of those dreams, she was didn't resist Jasmine's attempts of annoyance as she watched from the corner of her eye as she approached. Though she did quality work, she knew that Jasmine was coming for her. Being a lead Jasmine would let her know if there was an issue with an item that she's sent through and as she approached Kenya, she began to rant. "Ms. Palmer. As you know we expect a superior product here because I have advised you of that before!" Kenya turns to acknowledge Jasmine, listening nonchalantly Kenya quickly asked, "Are you finished, because I have work to do." Then whirled around to her work station. Grabbing her chair handle Jasmine whirled her back around so fast that her body leaned with the motion, getting directly her face exclaiming "I am not finish speaking with you Ms. Palmer!" all Kenya could think about was how Jasmine had whirled her chair around so fast that she had almost given her whip lash and those long fake nails that she was now snapping in her face. Before she knew it she had grabbed that colorful red wig that Jasmine was wearing and was holding it in her hand. Jasmine stood there with her platted hair that looked like multiple antennas pointing in all direction then grabbing for Kenya to put her in a hold till security is called. Kenya not even thinking about Jasmine's stature, being twice her size, all she could see was Jasmine's tight jean jumpsuit popping a few buttons as in one swift motion whirled around to avert her grasp resulted in Jasmine falling to the floor. Kenya quickly apologized and reached down to help her up grimacing as she thought about what she had just done, making sure that Jasmine was okay and dusting off her wig she handed it back to her, realizing that that not only was she about to lose her job but possibly about to face criminal charges, heart pounding hard and fast in her chest. By then security had arrived and escorted her to the office where she was sure the police would be coming soon to escort her out. There were no charges filed. Jasmine glimmer of a conscience and knowing how she'd mistreated and set Kenya up had achieved her mission and decided not to have her arrested, especially since she possibly could have been in trouble as well. Both regretful and embarrassed she marched her down the aisle with security at her side as onlookers some sneering but some looked more sympathetic because they'd heard and some observed how Kenya had been treated. Though disappointed at her handling of the situation was relieved at not having to go to jail. Getting into her car thinking to herself, now comes the hard part, she must now face Mr. and Mrs. Palmer. Deciding that she had enough of Cantonville that evening as she slowly drove home from work with tears filling her eyes as she made her mind up to enroll in the college of her original choice, which was Shannon's alma matter, Central State University in Hartmont, AL, only a couple of hours away from home, but close enough in case she needed her parents, and also only a couple of hours outside of the Atlanta in case she wanted to have some fun. She'd only enrolled "CCC" Cantonville Community College to please her parents. By the time she pulled up in the yard her tears had turned to laughter as she thought about Jasmine standing there with those plaits pointing in all directions like antennas as she stood there with Jasmine's wig in her hand. She didn't know whether she should try and place it back on her head or run. Laughing also out of the relief that no charges were filed because this could have resulted in a whole lot worse circumstances, and for that she was truly thankful and however ashamed she was at how she had conducted herself. Arriving home and slowly pulling into the driveway dreading what she'd have to face with her parents she hopped out of the car and ran straight to Olivia's room shutting the door behind her to fill her in on her firing and letting her know what her plans were for school. Olivia scolded her for giving in to her temper and letting something like this happen. She knew she would miss Kenya, since this would be the first time that they'd actually be apart, even if Olivia had been spending the majority of her time with her new boyfriend. Kenya waited to tell her parents after dinner, as Olivia glared at her and kicked her feet underneath the table while nudging her to go ahead and let them know what had happened. Sondra had already asked her if she was okay noticing that she didn't have much of an appetite, something strange for Kenya. She swallowed hard as she struggled to find the right words to say as she got their attention seeing they were getting ready to leave the table. That look of disappointment was too much for Kenya as she was no longer able to hold back the tears. They scolded her for her temperament, "Are you still fighting! I thought you had outgrown those days, and this time on the job." "Why can't you be more like your sister" Sondra blurted before she realized then taking a deep breath waved her hands as if to dismiss what she had just said, but Kenya heard it loud and clear and had always felt this way about the relationship between she and Sondra. Nathan gave Kenya a glimpse of sympathy regarding the comment but didn't seem shocked as if this was not a new revelation. Olivia looked on in embarrassment at what she'd just heard as Sondra and Nathan went on as if it had not been said letting her know that they supported her where ever she decided to go to college. Nathan let her know that he never want to have to see a news story because she was not able to control her emotions. At eighteen years, he didn't consider that the days of the spankings were over yet, but a talking to was as effective as a spanking when it came to Nathan. The next week Sondra drove Kenya to the campus of Central State a couple of hours away in Hartmont, AL. They had all the paperwork squared away as well as a dorm room for Kenya's first semester of college. Unfortunately she had not earned a scholarship like Olivia, but she was willing to find a job and go to work to help pay for her tuition.

The next weekend she moved into the dorm, which was a Sunday. Before taking off for the campus, she ran down the street to the Vincent's to say goodbye. As she rang the doorbell Myles answered as he gave her a brotherly hug and pretended to be glad to see her. He happened to be visiting that week end and let her know that he was only a couple of hours away from the campus and told her to let him know if she needed anything. This was a way for him to keep tabs on her from time to time as well. Sondra had already let Val know that Kenya was leaving. "Baby, I'm glad you came by here before you left for the campus because I made you some of my beignets to take with you, and had not had the chance to bring them to you, and Lord knows I don't need to eat them" she laughed as she rolled her hands over her stomach as she giggled and gave Kenya a hug before grabbing the tray wrapped with a fancy yellow bow and handed them to her. The thought of Val warmed her heart as she smiled at her and thought to herself that after all these years Mrs. Vincent has never lost that Creole accent as she thanked her for the beignets and expressed to her how much she would miss her. Especially those beignets, a lot of her foods were a little on the spicy side but Kenya had always loved Mrs. Vincent's cooking. She stopped in the den to say her goodbyes to Mr. Vincent, feeling compelled to give her advice as he walked her to the door with Val jesting with him to leave her alone with all the advice, as they laughed and gave her a hug as they watched her out the door and off to college.

Mr. Palmer was not able to make to trip due to his normal workaholic ways. Sondra accepted it saying "There could be a lot of other things that he could have taken up that would be a lot worse that working hard for the family." Even if she did have concerns, she wasn't about to air them to the girls. She wanted him to remain perfect in their eyes. They arrived into the quaint little college town and onto the gated campus with its plush greenery and well-structured buildings as they pulled up at Whitford Hall the women's dorm for freshmen and sophomores where Kenya would be staying. There happened to be a group of football players passing by, who were more than glad to help them with their luggage as they took notice of their rather attractive new comer to the campus. Kenya was naïve to their flirting so she ignored any advances, but it didn't get past Sondra, so she had her talk with Kenya as she took her to lunch after they'd gotten everything squared away in the dorm room. "Yes Mom, I already know all that," Kenya exclaimed as if she wanted to hush her, as she peered around the restaurant to see if there were any students around who may have been listening in. Although her father was her favorite, she was more like Sondra than not. Sondra could see many of her ways in Kenya and the two would have clashed if it wasn't for Nathan's intervention in many a circumstance. She drove Kenya back to the dorm as she nodded her head to Sondra's advice and they gave each other a big hug when they got out of the car. Yes Mom, I know you love me, I love you too." Sondra looked at Kenya and laughed, "You're going to appreciate my advice one day Kenya!" as she hopped in the car and drove away but didn't get too far before she was backing up to give her another hug. Kenya returned to her dorm room nervously anticipating the arrival of the young lady who would be her roommate. She'd already been there judging by the colorful sheets and comforter and obviously she loved stuffed animals. She wondered what she would be like and if they would even like one another as she turned on the television and peered out the window that overlooked the dorm entrance.

# Chapter 5

Kenya did well in college though she was not a straight A student like her sister but what she didn't make in grades she made up for it with determination and hard work. Following in Nathan's footsteps she decided on Mass Communications as a Major with a minor in English which made him very proud. The dorm was a new experience for Kenya. Something that Olivia didn't experience since she stayed home and commuted while at CCC and then went on to Larson University which were both right there in Cantonville. There were so many cultures and a diversity of students from all over at Central State. She made friends with a few International Students and learned about their cultures. Everything was new and fascinating to Kenya. Her roommate was a girl named Jenifer Faye Adams, from Lexington, KY, whose nickname was Jena. She had the opportunity to go home with her a couple of weekends. Jena was not as settled as Kenya and was somewhat of a party goer during her first semester. Kenya didn't get a car till her third year of college so Jena was her source of transportation during her freshman year and since she took her to the grocery store or the game, then she would feel obligated to go to the club with her afterwards. On one occasion Jena had been invited to a Frat Party. She was excited and as she hot curled her hair as she paced back and forth to Kenya's closet. "Oh no Kenya, you can't wear that! Looking Kenya up and down. "You dress like you came straight from a Convent. We're gonna need to go clothes shopping if you're gonna hang around me!" She sashayed back over to her closet and pulled out one of her dresses that was short black and mainly straps. Kenya being taller than Jena, was already getting an idea of how short this dress was going to be on her, however with a feeling of obligation, she tried the dress on. She slid the dress on and combed her hair down. The dress exaggerated every curve and was definitely as short as she thought it would be. Kenya was afraid that if she had to bend over she would not be able to hide anything at all. As Kenya stepped from behind the closet door Jena exclaimed "Kenya Girl, you look awesome! I'm so jealous! Who would have known you had a figure like that!" "Thank you Jena, but where is the rest of it!" Kenya laughed as she teased with Jena about her little short dress. "You know that as long as my legs are this dress is nothing but a blouse on me, and I can't be going out like that, I'm gonna wear my dress from the convent!" She said as she tugged at the bottom of the dress as she attempted to reach up to pull one of her own dresses out of the closet. "Okay!" replied Jena "but don't be mad when everybody is asking me to dance instead of you." she said as she flaunted her hips from side to side in her tight mustard yellow dress. Kenya didn't mind, because that was not the kind of attention that she was looking for anyhow, turning out to be more of a body guard for Jena that night since she tended to attract the rowdier of the bunch. On over into the night one of the Frat boys who'd been dancing with Jena had turned his attention to Kenya and had gotten verbal with her when she refused to continue to dance with him as he seemed to have too many hands as well as too many drinks. It was a good time to leave anyhow, with Jena having her fill of alcohol. Kenya ended up having to take Jena's keys from her and with her little driving experience in a stick shift, managed to get them back to the dorm safely. Kenya thought to herself if was a good thing that she was there with her because the night would have ended badly with the particular few in the crowd that Jena was drawing. Fortunately by the second year Jena had gotten it all out of her system and had had enough of the parties and clubs and was ready to focus a little more on her studies. She made good use of her dance skills on the football field by trying out and making the squad for the University's dancing team "The Tigerettes of Central State". That allowed spare time for Kenya but keeping in touch with the family was not something Kenya used it for, however she did try and make sure she was home for the holidays if the work schedule permitted. She would have Olivia to pick her up from campus when she was ready to go home being embarrassed to ask Jena to her home, with her with her coming from such a small city compared to Lexington's where Jena was from. The first three years Kenya worked at the campus book store, where she got more and more acquainted with books and writing. There were young men who would have liked become acquainted with Kenya, but she didn't pay them any attention with the exception of this one young man named Dillan Turner who caught her eye early on. She found herself becoming more of a bookworm, where in the past she had always excelled in sports but had stopped playing basketball in her Junior Year at Cantonville High School to concentrate on her studies.

# Chapter 6

She had been in constant contact with Olivia calling lately with her becoming engaged and wedding was during Kenya's junior year. She was marrying her college sweetheart Brian Langston, son of the city's Mayor. Brian had just become a police officer for the city of Cantonville. Apparently Kenya didn't have to do much talking when Olivia called, since she would call to get Kenya's opinion on the wedding, then would answer her own questions before Kenya could answer as she would rant on and on about the wedding. It was out of nervous excitement, but no thoughts of backing out. She and Brian was in love since elementary school, at least that's what Brian told her, she just didn't know it till they went away to college. Immediately after college, Brian had gone away to the Police academy, but they kept in touch and became inseparable. Olivia was always confident, smart, and knew exactly what she wanted out of life. Kenya did envy her a little with her perfect life however she didn't envy having to prepare for this wedding. Being more of an athlete, workout clothes and that long pony tail was more of Kenya's attire growing up. She wasn't into the hair, nails, makeup and fancy clothes as older sister Olivia, so getting dressed in the fancy bridesmaid dress and heels to participate in Olivia's wedding was quite an ordeal for Kenya. Kenya had taken a three day weekend and had come home on that Thursday evening for the wedding rehearsal and dinner. Seeing her come down the aisle like a baby deer, Olivia and the bridesmaids were having to give

Kenya a lesson in "How to Walk in Heels 101". When the fellas teased Kenya about her walk, Olivia replied as she laughed "Stop laughing at my sister you guys, she is going to learn to walk in those shoes and she will be a force to be reckoned with!"

Between Olivia, and Sondra feeling that she had a knack for decorating and full of ideas and advice, the wedding planner was barely able to get a word in as well, regardless, it turned out to be a beautiful wedding indeed. The colors she'd chosen were salmon pink and black. The silver trimmings of gave the place an extra touch of elegance with the bouquets of pink roses and silver ribbons. It was time for the wedding and the bridesmaids were sensational in their salmon pink dresses and they stood and took their places and the men in their grey tuxedos with striped salmon pink and black cummerbunds and ties, along with flower girls and ring bearer stood waiting for the arrival of the bride, but non anticipated the brides arrival more than the regal and handsome groom Brian as he stood there waiting nervous but ready. And as the wedding party stood waiting finally from behind the ivory curtains appeared the most gorgeous bride as the audience stood and turned toward the aisle. Olivia's gown was white lace trimmed with sequins and a long train that filled the isles. Her veil covered her forehead as she took Nathans arm as he lead her down the aisle, wondering if she would shake the all petals off of her bouquet as her hands trembled. It's amazing how much the two resembled as they walked arm and arm down the aisle as Sondra looked on proudly. She was a beautiful bride, skin chocolate brown and high cheekbones with teeth as perfect and white as the wedding dress she was wearing as she smiled until those big brown eyes began to fill with tears both nervousness and of joy as they approached the while Brian watched and admired this beautiful young woman whom he loved and was about to become his wife. Naturally Nathan was both proud and a little sad as he gave his oldest daughter away in marriage but was confident that Brian would take good care of Olivia. Pastor Newcomb sometimes tended to be a little long winded, as the crowd awaited for those words, "You may now kiss the bride." excited about celebrating a joyous occasion as a wedding ceremony and was equally anticipating the food and entertainment as they awaited once again as the wedding party made their entrance.

As the night went on, first dances, the toasts, the food, the throwing of the bouquet by the bride, the throwing of the garter by the groom and the cutting of the cake had taken place and all left now was the dancing and the booze, as the bride and groom mingled with the crowd. It didn't go un-noticed that Kenya had grown into a beautiful young lady as well. She bare more of a resemblance to Sondra with her golden brown complexion and almond eyes. The family members were curious as to whom Kenya was dating or when she would even begin. Brian's younger brother had always had a crush on Kenya, and throughout the evening she'd been avoided his glances, being a year younger than herself, she displayed no interest in him. Being in the wedding party with Kenya was a thrill for Teddy, he was just as bold as ever taking every opportunity to flirt with her, particularly when they finally had the chance to dance during which he took the opportunity to show her how well skilled he was with his hands. "Don't think I won't still spank you Anthony Theodore Langton" as she would call his by his whole name whenever he was in trouble with her and teased him that his name sounded presidential, "Move your hands back up!" "Spank me please!" He laughed, "I miss those days." "Teddy, your last whoopin from me was only a couple of years ago during your senior year of high school." Kenya replied. He had grown to be a rather fine and handsome young man himself and was now all muscle after being on the High School Football Team and going on to play for Paul at CCC. He was one of the star players and would possibly be going pro. Although, he had grown out of the baby fat he had affectionately earned the name Teddy, and the name was sticking with him, unlike Kenya, who had been attempting to avoid him all evening. Truth is Kenya was avoiding being hurt. During her freshman year she had fallen in love with a young man, Dillan Turner, who had lavished her with affection and treated her like a queen, then one day all of sudden told her that he did not want to see her anymore. It was hard for Kenya not to think of Dillan Turner when she thought of her sophomore year. There were some things that she has never uttered a word to anyone about her years at Central State and figured were better off left unsaid. She sat there at the table with the rest of the wedding party, pretending to be listening and as she laughed on que at their jokes and comments while she found her mind drifting a million miles away, reflecting back on a different time, when she and Jena had gone out on a double date with Dillan and his roommate Mylam. Jena and Mylam had gone into his suite and Jena just so happened to have driven them to the dorm where they gathered after their movie date. Kenya had no plans of spending the night but Jena had gotten too comfortable with Mylam and didn't seem to be coming out of the suite anytime soon. Kenya was a virgin and had no plans of giving up her virginity until she was married so she and Dillan just snuggled on the couch but after a few wine coolers she found herself getting very sleepy as she laid against Dillan's shoulder and had fallen asleep as they watched TV. The next thing she remembered was the sun was shining through the window of Dillan's dorm room as she lay underneath him naked. Confused and baffled but refusing to believe that he may have slipped anything into her drink last night, she thought to herself, maybe she had too many, but one thing she knew for sure was that he had been with her intimately because she was sore in places that she had never felt. After realizing what had happened she pushed him away awaking him as he reached over to grab and slid her next to him as he hugged her as he looked into her eyes and asked her what was the matter, as he kissed her forehead while he told her how much he cared for her and made her feel that everything would be okay. After knocking on the door to Mylam's suite and getting a muffled answer from Jena to go away, Kenya did what she should have done the night before and had Dillan to drive her back to her dorm. Things were back to normal until a couple of months later when she started to feel a little strange. In the mornings she would get up and make a dash for the bathroom or feel nauseated after eating. She could no longer stand the fragrance of perfumes or the scented lotions and the only thing that she could hold on her stomach was ice cream. She knew that she was pregnant and was so afraid and couldn't figure out how she would tell Dillan, and even more difficult how would she tell her parents. They would be so disappointed, especially Sondra, but at least she had Dillan, or so she thought. Within about a few days after discovering that she was pregnant she noticed that Dillan had started acting strangely, as if something was bothering him. Finally he called her one day and told her he couldn't see her anymore. Her heart nearly skipped a beat. She couldn't believe what she was hearing, pleading with him then blurting out "Dillan, you can't leave me now...I'm pregnant!" There was a silence on the line. He didn't know whether she was just now telling him because she was trying to trick him into staying with her, but regardless, he was more afraid now, and was not ready to be a father or for marriage and had at this point made up in his mind that he would leave regardless. All he could do was hang up. Even to that day, unknown to Kenya, Myles had been behind this break up as well as her firing. He'd follow up on Kenya from time to time and had found out about the young man that Kenya was dating, that he seemed to be a fine and upstanding gentleman. After finding out his name and phone number he had been anonymously making calls

him to with lies about her and was so desperate to see her suffer that
he ultimately paid the young man to break it off with her. The money
along with the fact that Kenya was pregnant was enough to run him
off. Kenya made calls to him with no answer or return. When she did
reach him he was pressuring her to have an abortion. She saw him
walking in a distance while she was leaving the library one day, this
time with a female with whom he seemed quite cozy with. Both hurt
and afraid for her future as well as her child's, she went to her dorm
room and covered herself under the covers not knowing what she
would do and still not knowing how she would break the news to her
parents, dreading to disappoint Sondra. Jena finally came over to the
bed and snatched the covers off her head noticing how swollen and
red her eyes were. Though she had her suspicions that Kenya may
have been pregnant she never mentioned it. "Come on Kenya come
to church with me in the morning, you know you can't lay in this bed
all day tomorrow crying over that jerk!" Going to church was
something neither of them had done since they had been at Central
State. The next morning they went to Calvary Baptist, which took in
a large number of college students since it was down the street from
the campus. Kenya tried to constrain herself but all she could do
during the service was cry. Embarrassed as she wiped her eyes and
nose while Jena patted her hand, she never figured herself to be one
of those who would be all emotional during the church service but
for the first time in her life she cried passionately as Jena sat there
wishing there was something more that she could do. That night as
she lay in bed Kenya noticed a warm wet sensation on her sheets,
realizing that she was starting to spot and although she knew what
was happening she tried to hide it from Jena, tipping into the
bathroom to call Olivia. Olivia concerned and wanting to drive down
right away but Kenya although she was afraid about what was
happening, not wanting to alert Sondra of any trouble, pleaded with
her to wait till morning that way their parents would not be alarmed
or suspicious and promised to call her if she took a turn for the worse.
Olivia showed up early that next morning after being worried all
night and upset but stayed calm and supportive for Kenya's sake, as
she gave her a hug and helped her to the car. Jena had already gone
to breakfast before class so Kenya was relieved that she didn't have to
explain anything. She just left her a note saying that she was going
home for a few days when in actuality she was in right there at
Harmont Memorial Hospital. Olivia could be pretty tough herself
and was able to track down Dillan to let him know that Kenya was in

the hospital. She let him know that her fiancée was a police officer, although he was not yet an officer and she knew that he would not be able to do anything about the situation, but yet and still was able to scare Dillan into taking care of the hospital bill. A couple of days later Kenya was released as Olivia had returned to Harmont to take Kenya back to the dorm. Looking concerned as she watched them entered the room, Jena asked "How was your trip?" still with her suspicions, knowing that Kenya would never stay in bed and this was not like her, even if she was heartbroken over Dillan. "It was good Jena! A much needed break." Kenya managed to smile to seem more convincing. "She is going to forget about Dillan in no time." Olivia answered. Jena brought Kenya some food from the cafeteria later that day when Olivia left and helped her catch up on some of her classwork. Olivia had left her with a few things as well that she would need, Jena noticing the large supply of sanitary items. Olivia never spoke a word to her parents about what had happened. Since Dillan was left with the hospital bill he tried getting in contact with Myles to get more money afterward but Myles had been using a track phone which he discarded each time he called him. Myles made a phone call a few weeks later to Kenya as if checking on her but had no idea how much she had really suffered. She was heartbroken over Dillan but would never forget the pain of losing her unborn child. As a getaway she absorbed herself into the books and her work. Whatever she did she did with a passion and determination.

   She took a swig of her champagne and shook off those thoughts as Teddy approached her at the table and asked if he could have one more dance before the night ended. She grabbed her glass and took one last gulp of champagne as Teddy took her by the hand and pulled her out to the dance floor, while she playfully scolded him about what would happen this time if he didn't control his hands, as the rest of the wedding party laughed and teased Kenya about having to get bare feet, however, she had learned to tackle those shoes.

# Chapter 7

Upon graduation Kenya had already started an internship during her senior year with one of the more prestigious news stations in the region, WASA TV, Chanel 7 and as soon as her internship was over the company was more than willing to offer her a permanent position as On-Air Reporter. Kenya's days following in Nathan's footsteps were paying off. She had the potential to be an award winning journalist. Not only was she beautiful and but intelligent and quick witted. It was hard to catch Kenya off guard. She had turned her bossiness and smart mouth around and let it work for her and was growing into a very successful young woman. For the first time she felt that Sondra was taking notice of her as she felt the sincerity when she let her know how proud she was of her. Nathan took the time out of his busy schedule as he and Sondra drove to Hartmont to celebrate Kenya's new job by taking her to lunch. They noticed that she already had somewhat of a fan based by all who seemed to recognize her while they were out. She was satisfied with settling there in Hartmont, the quaint little college town with its pleasant atmosphere which placed her within a couple of hours away from home as well as to other places that she liked visiting. She found herself growing accustomed to Hartmont, and the people there.

Kenya had a tendency to get too much into her stories and the reporters had been warned about getting too emotionally attached to her news stories and after nearly a year on the job found herself intrigued with a story she had done with a homeless veteran who had taken to the streets by choice and had been taking his check which he had sent to the address of one of the homeless shelters in the area where he once stayed, spreading it among the homeless community, sometimes doing without himself. He had been so organized that he and his crew had been challenging the criminals in the area and crime rates had actually gone down even more in that area. The crew had gone out to the area in where he stayed, which happened to be in an alley, downtown Hartmont, in a makeshift tent. This man could have been anyone's grandfather, and had she gotten to know hers, she figured she would want one like him. This was a war hero who had chosen to stay in the streets, still protecting others. She was so compelled to find him after work that she ended up going to a local restaurant to buy him a meal and take it to him. Thinking herself to be invincible as usual, she drove the street till she found the area that Mr. Billingsley was living. Figuring she would be in and out in no time she parked her car on the street and headed down the alley with the food that she had purchased for him catching the attention of a group of other homeless. She walked a little faster as she headed towards the section of the alley that Mr. Billingsley should have been located when she ran right into this bearded figure who seemed rather large and threatening. He looked at Kenya as he towered over her, casting a shadow and cornered her against the wall. He looked down at her as her chest heaved up and down as she stood there wondering if he could hear her heartbeat. His eyes trailed down to the food that she had in her hand for Mr. Billingsley. She swallowed deep and asked the man if he knew where Mr. Billingsley was. "Who's asking?" he replied in a very gruff tone with eyes like steel and a face that was expressionless as he stared down at Kenya. This moment seemed to be an eternity as Kenya met his stare and started to speak not knowing what this man's intentions were. She thought to herself she should have listened to her co-workers. She stuttered to answer as a voice rang out from the shadows, and she could see where Mr. Billingsley's tent was cast. "It's okay Little Joe," She breathed a sigh of relief, Little Joe, she thought to herself as she stared at this giant standing before her. "She's good people!" Mr. Billingsley laughed as he shuffled out. He'd just come from down the street dumpster diving, and was ready to show Kenya some of the things that he'd found. "That's Little Joe, Little Joe, as he seemed to have a habit of repeating himself. He gets a little riled up when new faces come around. He's another one of the protectors of our little community back here." "Little Joe!" she repeated loudly as if she were intending to say more as he turned and took another look at Kenya before walking back into his corner of the alley. Mr. Billingsley gave Kenya a scolding look as if he was speaking to his own child or one of his young soldiers, but never loosing that twinkle as if he was ever so glad to see her. "Young Lady what brings you out this time of the evening? Do you know what danger you could have been in?" "Come take a seat!" "Take a seat!" he goes on before she can answer, as he points towards his makeshift seat that had come from the back of an automobile. "I'm sorry Mr. Billingsley, I just wanted to come check on you and bring you some food." His eyes lit up as he takes the food from Kenya hand. Frail and a head full of grey hair, Kenya noticed during the interview he looked like he had not eaten in days. Mr. Billingsley shared his chicken, potatoes and biscuits with a few of the neighbors, which is one thing that was so accustomed to on the streets, even to his own hurt, as he introduced Kenya. She knew that he appreciated every bit of it by the way he was crunching on the bones. They sat there and talked for a while as Mr. Billingsley neighbors noticed and figured that Kenya was good people if Mr. Billingsley allowed her to sit and talk. Kenya found out things that he'd kept hidden during the earlier interview, that he was originally from Tennessee and his real name was Frank Watkins. He did let her know during the earlier interview that he was retired as a Captain in the Army and had lost his wife, as she'd learned in her earlier interview, about 15 years ago and had become a wonderer and ended up in Hartmont, AL of all places. "Don't you have any children Mr. Watkins, I mean Mr. Billinglsey?" Kenya asked again, since he avoided the question during the interview, but Mr. Billingsley purposely avoided the question once again. "Well it's getting late now young lady and you need to be heading home. Thank you for coming back to check on an old man like me!" Kenya naturally had the mind of an interviewer and had become so fascinated and concerned with Mr. Billingsley. There was still so much that she wanted to know about him. She asked if he minded if she came to visit him from time to time. He let her know that these alley is not a place for a young lady like herself, but didn't really try to dissuade her because he loved the company. As she walked back down the alley, she noticed that Little Joe had come out of his corner and started to slowly follow behind her, she started to speed up but she realized that though he seemed intimidating that this time he was in protective mode again but was actually watching over her as she walked through that alley. She realized that so many things could have gone terribly wrong but she just had to see Old Mr. Billingsley again. She waved to Little Joe as she hopped in her car and drove off. The next day she arrived at work and dared not mention where she had gone the day before. A couple of weeks later while cooking herself a meal and thinking to herself as she sat there alone, why am I sitting here alone with this food when someone else would enjoy this meal with me scooping up all she had left over and heading back to that same alley where she found Mr. Billingsley. His eyes lit up when he saw her coming. She'd even brought enough for little Joe this time. They sat and enjoyed their meal as she watched Mr. Billingsley's seemed to come to life as he told stories of his wife Mariam and their life together, she laughed and shed a tear or two till it was time for her to be escorted out of the alley by Little Joe. This started to be a weekly routine for Kenya as she affectionately began to call him Gramps. She didn't have many friends in Hartmond besides her friends from the alley. Kenya would make sure she'd cook enough food for Mr. Billingsley's neighbors as well as they sang and danced and shared their stories. Such an unlikely bunch of friends. Her co-workers at the station often wondered how Kenya spent her free time. A couple of the females who'd been giving her a hard time since she was new to the crew decided that they would follow her one evening to see what she does with her time. Trailing behind and noticing where she parked they figured maybe she's just going into some of these restaurants because there is nothing in this part of town, and she was, however she came out with enough food to feed an army. This definitely got their attention. Sometime later they passed by the area again and noticed that Kenya's car still parked as they saw her coming out of the alley, they turned around and pulled up beside her as she was getting into her car. Tiffany rolled the window down glaring at Kenya as she asked "What are you doing out here in this alley alone?" "Are you crazy? You're gonna get yourself mugged or killed out here! Wait, There's nobody back here but the homeless. I'll bet you're visiting the homeless Vet that you did a story on a while back!" Kenya's heart beating fast as she rushed to get into her car. "Don't worry about me, what are you two doing in this area?" as she hopped in her car and sped off. She was a nervous wreck knowing that her job may be in jeopardy, already being warned about following and becoming attached to her stories. As she got ready for bed she rehearsed and thought about what she would say if she were to be confronted and called into the manager's office. When the alarm clock went off the next morning she dreaded going in to the station but got her shower, pulled herself together and headed out to the car, still thinking about what she would say while she drove that 20 minute drive to work. Walking down the long corridor and into her office, she started her normal routine as she got her morning coffee and checked her email then prepared herself for the story of the day and just as she did the two who had confronted her on the evening before entered her office and shut the door behind them as they stared at her and she tried to stare the two of them down. They were inseparable and may as well had been twins because it seemed when one moved the other moved. She knew they had each other's back. "May I help you?" Kenya asked as if nothing had happened. "Oh, you know why we're here." Replied Felicia Graham as Tiffany Wright looked on. "Seems like you've become attached to that story haven't you?" She went on, as Tiffany cut in "I knew it was something about you." As they rolled their eyes at one another then at Kenya. Felicia rolled her eyes toward Tiffany replied "I can tell by the way she walked up in here." Kenya stood there speechless waiting for them to call the manager in at any moment. Tiffany goes on "Yes, there is something about you." "You have a heart, I knew it was in there somewhere!" Kenya's mouth dropped open as Felicia and Tiffany began to laugh out loud. You mean you two are not about to report me and get me fired. "No!" laughed Felicia, "but you're gonna get yourself fired or hurt if you keep following your news stories like that!" "He's not just a story" replied Kenya. "We know that." replied Felicia "but you sure better be careful. "You've been giving us a tough time trying to keep an eye out for you!" added Tiffany. "Girl, you should have seen how big your eyes got!" laughed Felicia, as Kenya breathed a sigh of relief and joined in on the laughter. From that moment on the three were inseparable. She was supposed to let them know the next time she went to visit with Mr. Billingsley, but she grabbed the food she cooked for him and his neighbors and drove on out to that part of town, having an uneasy feeling that evening as she headed out. Making her way through the alley she notice that there was no sign of Little Joe but rounding the corner she noticed that he was sitting outside of Mr. Billingsley's tent. Little Joe rarely spoke but turning to her and said "He's not doing well today." Sitting the food down and taking a look at Mr. Billingsley she called his name but got no response. He was sweating and as hot as an oven. We're gonna have to get him some help. "I don't know who's going to help him" replied Little Joe. Kenya took out her phone to dial 911. She had given him the location and when the ambulance finally arrived and had gotten him to the hospital they tried to give them problems because he was homeless and didn't have an address, but because they recognized Kenya and did not want a story about the death of a homeless man because they turned him away they went ahead and admitted him. Kenya used her tech savvy to get in touch with his nearest relative, who happened to be a son, Franklin Jeffrey Watkins II. When Kenya arrived at work the next day she let Felicia and Tiffany know what had gone on, and later that evening after work she went back to Hartmond Memorial Hospital to check on Mr. Billingsley. She arrived to find a man in the room with Mr. Billingsley, a heavy set man of medium height and a rather distinguished look "You must be Kenya" as he smiled and walked towards her with extended arms. "Yes I am. How is he?" "I'm sorry" Kenya went on "where are my manners. Yes I am Kenya and you must be Mr. Franklin Jeffrey Watkins II." Yes I am and my father is going to be just fine, thanks to you. It was gall stones. No need to apologize. I'm just glad that he had someone like you to watch over him this way". Kenya didn't have to worry about being reported because this time it was the hospital who had recognized Mr. Billingsley from the interview and had called the station. Mrs. Stanfield decided that they would have Kenya to do a follow up interview. The story went nationwide. Kenya was about to lose her best friend whom she affectionately called Gramps. He would be going back to Memphis to stay with his son and family. She learned during the interview that the family had lost touch him and had been searching for him as he intentionally avoided his children because he didn't want to be a bother to them, wanting to be independent. Turns out he had two other sons and a daughter, and was Gramps to seven. Mr. Billingsley and his son had had a long talk and he was satisfied with going back with his son so Kenya was satisfied as well that he would no longer be on the street. They made sure that they went back to visit with the neighbors in the alley before leaving, this time it was with the news crew, though Kenya would have preferred this to have been a private moment. The station celebrated Kenya and her news story as the station ratings sky rocketed after hearing about how Mr. Billingsley had been reunited with his family. The family back in Cantonville called to congratulate Kenya for her achievement. This was a proud moment, especially for Nathan, but there was someone watching who wasn't so happy for her.

Through her career Myles followed Kenya's work and grew to despise her more the more successful she became, unable to deal with the fact that she'd had the opportunity to live her life but Chloe had to die. Feeling that he should have controlled the outcome of Chloe's death, he now felt compelled to control the outcome of Kenya's life. Although he had no desire to end her life, he wanted to destroy her in so many other ways and didn't want to be deprived of being able to watch it happen. He thrived on ways to torture her mentally, and seemed to get such enjoyment after watching her first romance crash and burn that he decided to pay one of his lovers to convince her of a whirlwind romance that would sweep her off her feet and cause her to fall so blindly in love before she can realize her ruin. He looked forward to setting her up for a big wedding for everyone to see, then watch her embarrassment and hurt after being dumped at the altar. What a news story that would be! And he knew just the man for the job, handsome, smart, and fine. He was into working out as Kenya was but the thing that convinced him that he would do it was the fact that this man loved money almost as much as he did. After all, he had paid him for much less while putting money even before his reputation, so doing this thing to Kenya, he was pretty sure, would not faze him. This man had moved into the area about two years ago from Philadelphia, Pennsylvania and worked at the Atlanta Stroudman and Marcus, so he made his contact and all was agreed. Stephon Smith was a chameleon. All past traces of the gang history and as a troubled youth as Steven he was able to escape, and embrace his inner self, and although female wasn't his type, for the money that Myles was offering he had no problem pretending, neither was there any problems with job relocation to the Stroudman and Marcus in the Hartmont, AL. Immediately they began to plot out how their paths would cross. Myles called her pretending to be a friendly check in and congratulating her on her news story while he delved to find out what her plans were for the week. She mentioned a restaurant that she would probably be visiting on Friday evening. He also knew that she worked out faithfully every Saturday Morning. Myles let Stephon know which restaurant to be at and had shown him pictures of her as well. She being a well-known public figure in the area he knew exactly who to look for, as he sat a distance away from the station but close enough to watch her as she left work for the restaurant was able to enter immediately after her to making sure that the waitress sat him directly across from where she was seated. He smiled at her and gave a little waved from across the aisles, building up the courage to approach her, telling her she looked lonely and asked if she would mind if he joined her, no sooner than he began the conversation Felicia and Tiffany arrived. She thanked him but let him know that she'd already had company for dinner pointing at her two friends approaching. Taking notice of his physique as they walked up behind him the two were all smiles. As he returned to his seat across the aisle, every attempt made to flirt from across the aisles went ignored by Kenya, although Felicia and Tiffany took notice as they teased Kenya about her rather attractive admirer. He called the waitress over to pay for his meal as he left immediately after Kenya and her co-workers, walking slowing behind the group till there was no doubt that he was interested in Kenya and would like an opportunity to talk to her. Felicia and Tiffany took the hint when they noticed him tagging along behind like a lost puppy. They giggled like school girls as they peered over their shoulders at Kenya's reaction to them as they walked away while she is approached by her handsome admirer. He was able to catch up with her before she got into her car. Felicia and Tiffany had ridden together and was watching from a distance to see what the outcome would be. Kenya let him know that she wasn't looking for a relationship and was content by herself. Obviously another attempt to avoid being hurt again. The look of disappointment as he returned to his car was enough for Felicia and Tiffany to draw their own conclusions, and Tiffany calling Kenya's cell as soon as he walked away, scolding her as they drove away, for rejecting such an attractive man without giving him a chance. Felicia and Tiffany nicknamed her the "Ice Princess" and ended their conversation as Felicia dropped Tiffany off at home. Stephon was on the phone as well. His conversation was with Myles, letting him know of the uneventful evening, but the next day was Saturday and that meant that he would be ready to try his hand again at the gym.

Myles had purchased Stephon a membership at the gym where Kenya was a member and he was parked down the street from Kenya's home around 9am that Saturday morning, knowing that was normally around the time that she headed to the gym noticing that she was coming out with her gym bag. He took off to the gym so that he'd already be there when she arrived, which was perfect with her running back inside because she'd forgotten her phone. By the time she got there Stephon was already in place. Purposely picking an area nearest the entrance he was pretending not to notice her but she definitely noticed him. He was into working out and it showed as she walked slowly pass taking in the view and thinking to herself, new face, hmmm wonder if his mind is as beautiful as that body of his. He had his back to her but she realized that this was the gentlemen that she'd seen the day before. Although she realized that she wasn't so nice to him the day before, she waved in his direction and attempted to get his attention. He pretended to be into his music and his work out and this time he wasn't noticing her. This time he was playing hard to get as he smiled to himself noticing that she was admiring his body. Kenya had no knowledge of how to flirt but tried working out near the areas that he'd occupy so that he may notice her. She was starting to feel worn out just attempting to get his attention, so finally about 30 minutes into her workout she'd built up her courage and was bold enough to approach him. She waltzed over and gently tapped him on the shoulder. He pretended to be surprised as he turned and smiled taking his ear buds out as she replied "Remember me?" She thought to herself that may not such a good thing. Stephon laughed "Why as a matter of fact I do remember you! Aren't you're the lady who gave me the cold shoulder at the restaurant!" She apologized for being so dismissive. They both laughed as he complimented her athletic physique and asked if she would like a work out partner. They worked out a little while longer before they both decided to call it a day. He asked if she would mind if he walked her to her car and jokingly gestured as if he was afraid to ask, as he suggested they exchanged phone numbers. Stephon was now ready to set the plans in motion. He let her know that he was the new manager of the men's department at Stroudman and Marcus, was new in town, had grown a little bored and would appreciate it if she could show him around sometimes if she wasn't busy. Kenya thought to herself that he was such a gentleman as she laughed and exclaimed that she would love to be his tour guide. She went on to ask if he knew Myles, as his heart skipped a beat. "Yes, but I can't say that I know him personally." I've met him briefly during our store visits in Atlanta. I've heard he was a real jerk." "I'm sorry, I don't want to offend you if he is a relative of yours or something." He exclaimed as he put his hand over his mouth. "No," Kenya laughed he was my neighbor in Cantonville, MS. Don't worry, she laughed. I won't tell him and I've heard pretty much the same. That he was very strict and regimented. Much of a power thing. As she went on. "If it bothers you I won't even mention that I know you!" she laughed. "Thank you!" He replied as he laughed off his nervousness.

Not only was he able to manage a phone number, but scored what he called a first date. He strolled back to his car with a huge smile and feeling accomplished as he could not wait to call Myles so that he could let him know of his accomplishment for the day. He let him know that he had to tell Kenya that he didn't know him and he'd heard that he was a jerk as they both laughed and he talked about the way Kenya was drooling at the mouth over his physic, and how goofy she was while attempting to get his attention while he ignored her. "I knew she wouldn't be able to resist when she saw that fine body of yours!" Exclaimed Myles as they laughed together. Stephon didn't want to seem too anxious or desperate, but he knew he had to win her over quickly, so they talked on the phone nearly every day till the date, and he told her all the things that he knew she wanted to hear. He could easily relate to her because he knew exactly how he would like to be treated by his lovers. He loved being pampered and made to feel special. Kenya was enjoying being in a conversation with a man whom she felt actually listened and understood her so well. Within just those few days, she was giddy and the whole office could tell the difference in her demeanor as she had told her besties Felicia and Tiffany all about their conversations and their upcoming date. Wednesday evening rolled around and Kenya excited and a little nervous, rushed home from work so she could get dressed to show Stephon around the town, she took off her dress and heels and slipped into something more comfortable. She found a blouse that was more flattering to her figure, she didn't have large breast but what she had was very noticeable particularly in the blouse that she had chosen. She found some comfortable jeans that also complimented her curves along with some flats that would be appropriate for walking. Both Tiffany and Felicia approved and would be waiting to hear from her about her date. They were aware of how long it had been since Kenya had even gone out with a man so they were hoping that all went well for Kenya because she deserved someone nice.

# Chapter 8

Stephon was fitting in well at the local Stroudman and Marcus, as a matter of fact he was fitting in exceptionally well with one particular young man named Jeff in the Men's Department who was said to be working his way through college, so Stephon normally stayed a little later to help him freshen up the in the Men's Department, but on today he was out of the door on time, and Jeff took notice as he watched him head out towards the back office before getting ready to leave for the evening. There were plenty of interested females in the store, some of whom he flirted so not to give away his male preferences. He headed out the door in a hurry to meet Kenya at a local restaurant Vandito's an Italian style restaurant in which they would dine once they finished the so called tour. Kenya was already there so parked his Mercedes and he hopped in the car with Kenya as she pulled out of the parking lot into street. They rode around town and listened to music as she showed him the sights and what made Hartmont special, before they headed back to the restaurant. Myles would take every opportunity he could to rub her hands as she shifted gears, she seemed to like it and at one point that she'd rested her hand on the panel while he reached over and held her hand. She seemed happy. Myles had given Stephon a credit card for his use so he didn't mind splurging. When mentioning the various restaurants in the area over the phone, he chose one of the finest restaurants in the city in efforts to impress Kenya. They had a wonderful time at dinner.

An ice cream shop was next door so he even suggested going for ice cream afterwards. They were like giddy school kids as they grabbed their ice cream and went for a stroll in the park which was adjacent the shopping center that the restaurant was in. It turned out be a very romantic date and were told on one occasion by an elderly couple of what a lovely couple they made. Although they weren't an official couple and this wasn't supposed to be an official date, she had the best time that she'd had in years just talking and acting silly together. She loved the fact that he seemed to accept her weird quirks and all. She felt that she could be herself with him. He walked her to her car before the end of the evening and gave her a warm hug and a kiss on the cheek and thanked her for his tour. She couldn't wait to get back home so that she could call Tiffany and Felicia as they often did with a three way call when there was something exciting or important to tell and she couldn't wait to fill them in on her wonderful evening with Stephon, and he couldn't wait to fill Myles in on all her silly quirks that she thought that he'd accepted and how he'd swept her off her feet with him.

"Why didn't you tell me she snorted like that when she laughed Myles! I told her it was cute, but that could be downright annoying! I mean, she seemed so refined until she started laughing." exclaimed Stephon as he and Myles laughed and he talked about how Kenya although tended to ignore it but seemed to get a little bothered when the waitress was overly flirtatious towards him and barely addressed her. He said that all of Kenya emotions showed in her face and he wished that she'd eaten a hot pepper when she'd ran out of water just so that he could see the look on her face. Though he had no interest in women, he was seemed to know exactly how to use women against each other and was a pro with the subtle flirting which he would use it as a way to go to get under Kenya's skin. This was not his first time faking a romance with a woman. He had been paid off before as he had recorded sex with a woman, in which he blurred is face, then posted to ruin and publicly embarrass a high profile female running for office. He had many tricks up his sleeve to keep Myles entertained. Kenya didn't pursue the issue with the overly flirtatious waitress because she was more intrigued with Stephon's conversation, but it humored him and would be the perfect entertainment for future dates. A little tension here, a little stress there, disguised in a smile and a good time. It can't be obvious and he would have to work fast because their intentions are to sweep her off her feet for the big wedding date in 6 months and set the stage for the runaway groom before she even knows what hit her, so that he could get back to normal life in Atlanta and back to Myles.

# Chapter 9

Within the first month there wasn't a day that they didn't see each other and still talked on the phone for hours. Parts of those conversations were recorded or had Myles on the other end, as they would laugh and mock her afterwards. Stephon had been filled in by Myles regarding Kenya's likes and dislikes. He knew her favorite hangouts, style of music and favorite foods. One evening he fixed Kenya dinner at his place with wine and candles and asked if she would mind if they pursued a more serious relationship. He mentioned to her that he would not pursue her sexually because he felt that it was such a sacred thing and would be more special if they waited for the right time. He had become a master of lies and deception throughout his life and was working his magic with Kenya. He explained to her that he had been celibate after a bad relationship that he had come out of. She felt for him after hearing his story of how his ex-girlfriend had broken his heart. She said yes to his request for a more serious relationship because she had totally fallen for him and could not believe how in touch he was with her feelings. She felt as if she'd met her soul mate and shared these things in phone conversations with Olivia who was a little suspicious and always protective of her little sister. She let her know that she was waiting to meet this mystery man who had stolen her heart.

Kenya invited Stephon to a company picnic and he played out the subtle flirting to the hilt which went over well with the women at Kenya's office. Kenya took notice of the attention that Stephon got from the females at the Station. She knew Stephon to be very personable and in her eyes he could do no wrong. Now the women on the other hand was a different story in Kenya's mind, as she watched Terri, one of the staff, pass by as she eyed Stephon and gave him the sweetest little wave as she walked past without acknowledging that Kenya existed. Kenya ignored her as well, as she tried being sensible to prove that she wasn't the jealous type. Afterwards he started stopping by unannounced while on his lunch hour to spend time with Kenya and had made himself very popular with her office staff, knowing exactly which ladies to target for a reaction. One day he made sure that she noticed as he exchanged phone numbers with some of the ladies on the office staff. The ladies began to say things to Kenya that would make her think that they knew her conversations with Stephon. She just shook it off and kept going as a way to keep the peace. Shortly afterwards, it was suggested by one of the staff that Kenya follow up on a news story which turned out to be very similar so Chloe's drowning. Kenya could not keep a straight face and broke down during the interview. She started to feel a little paranoid, but shook it off as well. Although the manager advised that it was unprofessional, she let her know that it had gone over well with some of the viewer and made her seem more caring, but advised her, no more displays of emotion. Myles had watched the interview and congratulated Stephon on a job well done. Stephon was enjoying the attention, even if Kenya was feeling a bit disrespected, but that was the point. Some of the ladies who tended not to associate with Kenya would come around when Stephon came into the office and only direct their conversations to him while ignoring Kenya as they stood there in her office. He was overly friendly just to see Kenya's reaction as she pretended not to be bothered, so when a few of the ladies suggested he be their personal trainer he took them up on their offers. Saturday work outs were not only she and Stephon, but at least 3 of the ladies from the office staff all vying for Stephon's attention. He wanted to ruffle Kenya's feathers but at the same time, didn't want to run her off, so he knew the exact moment to turn his charm on with Kenya, if she seemed to get a little frustrated with the situation, and would shower her with attention in front of ladies. He'd win her over with a gift or dinner afterwards and thank her for being so patient with him to reel her back in. He was definitely playing a challenging mental game. Stephon laughed when in conversation with Myles about how he would love to see a cat fight with the ladies at the station. He showed her such a good time and seemed so genuine when they were alone that she didn't complain, although she definitely took notice. Tiffany and Felicia took notice as well and when they confronted Kenya, she dismissed it and chalked in up to Stephon being a people person and women taking notice of the new man in town and them being a little jealous, and as gorgeous as Stephon is she could see how they would be and said to herself that she couldn't blame them. They decided that If Kenya was happy then so were they.

She loved his spontaneity. Soon Sunday became the day that they would spend every moment together, which was an issue that Sondra would discuss with her, sensing that she was starting to drift away and would stress to Kenya in their phone conversations, but Kenya would quickly avert the conversation. Sondra knew that prayer was the best thing she could do since Kenya had to make her own decisions. Stephon would surprise her with roses at the office. Every Saturday night after he got off work it was dinner or a movie and was sure to schedule himself off for their Sunday road trip. Her friends waited on Monday to hear about what they'd done for the weekend. They also enjoyed the simple things as well when they would sit at home, relax and still have a good time something as simple as a movie at home. Truth is, Stephon was doing those things that he'd like to do since he could do them with Myles's money. He was definitely a charmer and would always win her over with his conversation although the tension at the office, all the sideways glances and glares soon started to get under Kenya's skin and distract her from her work and was very noticeable. She didn't associate any of it with Stephon, while he was drawing her closer to him but causing division on her job. All she could think of was that she had finally found a man who was not just after her body but thought she was worth waiting for so she was convinced that he was perfect and could do no wrong, and he took full advantage of the situation at his attempts to ruin her, or perhaps he would cause her to ruin herself. Kenya began to be so distracted with all the tension that she started making simple errors that she would not normally make to the point of being called into the manager, Mrs. Veronica Stansfield's office after an oversight on a story that she'd done. She knew that it had to be pretty serious for Mrs. Stansfield who rarely travels outside of her office area to stop by her office door and signal for her to follow her. As she locked her computer from the story that she was working on and went quickly down the hallway to be that person on the other side of Mrs. Stanfield's desk, which is a dreaded thing. As she walked in Mrs.

Stansfield asked her to shut the door behind her while being cordial and asking Kenya how she had been doing, as Kenya answered and made small talk, leading up to the reason for what she had actually been called into the office about. Mrs Stansfield was a good natured woman. She had a good sense of humor and very quick witted as Kenya is, but she gave that same over the rim look that reminded her of Sondra when she was serious about a matter, except Mrs. Stansfield actually wore glasses, and wore them on the end of her nose, as she starred at Kenya with Kenya wondering if she could hear her swallow. "You know I love you and I love your work Kenya. You are the baby of the bunch and you make me proud with the little experience that you have you have such talent. But you are starting to make many errors. Now, I know you're in a new relationship and a little distracted but we can't let this keep happening, so please stay focused, baby girl." which was a nick name that she had given Kenya with her being the newest to the crew and just out of college. "The other day you called an assailant by the name of the victim, unfortunately the piece had already aired before we were able to catch it. The family of the victim were upset so we need you to go on air and acknowledge the correction and apologize to the family and the viewers during your next broadcast." She exclaimed as she watched Kenya's expressions. Kenya had learned to be humble though out the years and there was nothing left for her to do except quickly agree and apologize as she promised that it wouldn't happen again as she thanked her for giving her another chance. She found herself paying more attention to what was going on around her lately rather than on her work at hand. Particular staff members who were friendly with Stephon and didn't mind rubbing it in Kenya's face. Myles had been filled in by Stephon to tune in to watch the broadcast, he couldn't have felt more proud, as he sat there in his living room smiling harder than a Cheshire cat. The family called afterwards, even Sondra was supportive and let Kenya know that they had watched to stay focused and everything was going to be alright and Stephon of course played the supportive role, as she let him know how very lucky she was to have a man like him by her side. Stephon knew that she'd fallen hard and he was the perfect distraction to get her thrown off course. Slowly he was destroying her for Myles's sake, and Myles couldn't have been more thrilled.

# Chapter 10

One evening Kenya and Stephon were relaxing at Kenya's watching a movie when she decided to wash her hair and decided that she would multi-task and do laundry at the same time. As she went to get a towel from the laundry room, noticing the hair remover in the cabinet along with the shampoo, Stephon quickly poured half the shampoo out and poured hair remover into the shampoo bottle before she could reenter the room. As she began to wash and rinse she was shocked at the handfuls of her long tresses that were coming out and screamed as she exclaimed "I must really be stressing more than I realized!" "Look at my hair!" she screamed as Stephon ran into the bathroom where she stood with patches of hair missing, as he tried to hold in his laughter. He cleared his throat and tried to look surprised while sneaking a recording with his cell phone to send to Myles of Kenya crying while she was holding one of her long tresses in her hand. "There are handfuls of my hair coming out right now." she pouted as Stephon acted concerned and helped her rinse and towel dry. He gave her a big hug before leaving that night and told her he loved her regardless of what her hair looked like. They looked at one another in surprise, because that was actually the first time that he told her he loved her. All of a sudden she was no longer crying because of her hair, but because the man she'd fallen head over heels for told her he loved her. She looked him in his eyes through those tears as she began to laugh as wrapped her arms around his neck and he reached around her waist and pulled her close to him as she told him that she loved him too. All of a sudden her mind was no longer on her hair but the fact that she had someone in her life who loved her unconditionally. The next morning he made an early call to her and said he wanted to come over she left for work. Bringing breakfast he convinced her that he wanted to see how she was doing. He watched her reaction as he decided to test the waters, jokingly suggesting that they take the day off and just go to the courthouse to get married. Giddy at the fact that he would even suggest marriage. "We can't just jump up and get married Stephon, we have to plan things out!" Kenya laughed and could not stop smiling. "Just kidding Honey, I know that" laughed Stephon. She wore that smile for the rest of the day. When Stephon gave Myles a call that evening they laughed hysterically as he told Myles what he'd done and how Kenya reacted to those patches of missing hair as she stood there with those clots of hair in her hand and went on to tell him about his suggestion of marriage. He exclaimed "She would marry me in a minute, I'll bet that even with those patches of missing hair, she'll have that same silly smile on her face when she had when she goes on air today. You need to tune in to see!" laughed Stephon. Myles laughed hysterically "You have marriage in her head now Stephon, that's probably all she can think about on that news cast. If she's asked a question, all she'll be able to answer is "Yes!" "She probably can't wait for you to ask her again! Heck, she'll probably ask you!" Stephon went on as they laughed together before ending their conversation.

As Kenya arrived at the office the stares were enough to let her know that the missing hair was very noticeable. She was to go on air for the evening spot, so Felicia and Tiffany swooped her out to the Style and Essence Salon that they all three used and when Zeta her stylist saw her hair, she took her in right away. The patches weren't as extreme as they looked and Zeta was able to style her hair in such a way that they weren't noticeable since she refused the weave and hair pieces. Seeing Kenya's new look made Felicia want to get rid of her long weave for a short do. Tiffany even agreed but would probably cry as she watched her long blonde tresses fall to the floor, she flashed her big blue eyes at them and exclaimed that she would just settle for a perm for now, but no drastic changes for her. Kenya returned to the office that afternoon with a new look, cut and color. This would take a little for Kenya to get used to because she had always worn long hair that she could throw into a pony tail at her convenience, but gone were those days. She received many compliments from her co-workers as well as the viewers. When Stephon met her at the station that evening after her news cast, though he was the culprit, he was surprised and pleased at Kenya's new look.

The next day was a day for the girls to hang out and while they were hanging out in Kenya's room she happened to mention her shampoo as Felicia took a look at the bottle of shampoo in Kenya's hand sniffing it exclaimed "This smells awful!" as she chunked the shampoo into the trash. "Never use that brand again girlfriend!"

# Chapter 11

Kenya was beginning to love the new look and taking on a new spark about her. She hurried home from work and changed clothes for date night with Stephon. He was taking her somewhere special tonight, so she made sure she wore something nice. When he showed up he gave her a big hug and kiss then opened the car door for her as a gentleman would. Arriving at the restaurant the attendant parked the car and as they walked inside Kenya felt like royalty in this elegant restaurant. She would get an occasional glance because she was a local television personality and Stephon being a new face in town, handsome and successful, would have full attention of the staff, however on this particular night the staff's glances were because they had been made aware of the couple's arrival and had been waiting to escort them to their table. Kenya noticed that they seemed to have the best seat in the restaurant and outstanding service. As they finished their entrée, the server arrived with the desert tray Kenya noticed that they had full attention as the staff gathered, "It's not my birthday" she turned to Stephon, and the server lowered and opened the dessert tray it held a tiny black jewelry box. Kenya began to cry as Stephon took the ring as the server lowered the tray. He opened the box through the candle light revealed a bright shiny new diamond ring as he got down on one knee at Kenya's lap. She sat there speechless as Stephon asked "Kenya Alexis Palmer, will you please marry me?" looking intently into his eyes she managed through her tears a "Yes!" She turned to notice through the dimmed lights that some of the office staff were seated at the tables surrounding them and a camera man was even filming the proposal, as the patrons burst into applause Felicia and Tiffany came over to give her a hug and congratulate her. Stephon had asked for Felicia and Tiffany's help with his proposal idea. She would rather it had been something more private and didn't understand why he always wanted to be so public with everything, but couldn't believe all the good things that were happening in her life right now. Unfortunately He was setting her on a very high pedestal before she comes crashing down. Kenya was beaming the next day at the office which was a Friday, so they had planned a trip to Cantonville that weekend to celebrate their engagement with their family. Kenya realized she didn't know anything about Stephon's family except what he'd told her, but she was that she had to be the luckiest woman in the world to have been swept off her feet by this wonderfully intelligent and attractive man. She was in love. Of course Stephon had no plans of introducing her to any of his family. He quickly dismissed any mentions of trips to meet his family in Philadelphia. He kept mentioning that schedules would not allow on such short notice and he would fly his parents out on day before the wedding. They planned a wedding date of June 25th, which was literally around the corner since it was now April. The family was glad to finally meet Stephon and was very welcoming. He had learned how to charm throughout the years. He'd come a long way since his days of gang fights, but was still a hustler, the only difference was that he was now wearing a business suit and hustling a different crowd. By now Olivia had a 16 month old and Kenya was glad to get home to spoil her little niece Kyla Shae, with whom she had been neglecting lately with all the attention that she'd been showering on Stephon. Kenya brought her a couple of little outfits and as she tried them on, one of which became her favorite outfit and she wouldn't allow Olivia take it off. Olivia exclaimed to Stephon that she couldn't wait for him and Kenya to have kids so she could come over spoil them then go home. She may have made small talk with him however there was something about Stephon that just didn't go over well with Olivia and the tension was apparent in the way that they interacted with one another. Kenya would intercede when she noticed that the conversation would become a little tense between the two and before Olivia would ask him too many questions regarding his past she would quickly change the subject. Olivia would intentionally mispronounce his name by calling him Steven instead of Stephon,

ironically Steven Smith happened to be his real name that he grew
up with on the streets of Philadelphia. There happened to be a few
arrests back when he was a Juvenile, and although many people called
him Steven, somehow the fact that Olivia called him Steven made
him a little nervous. Even Brian noticed the tension between the
two, but just passed it off as she being the over protective big sister,
however it caused him to pay closer attention to Stephon. Stephon
breathed a sigh of relief as Sondra finally stepped into the den to
let everyone know that dinner was ready and as they all headed to
the dining room, Kenya quickly side stepped between the two to
be careful that Olivia was not seated near Stephon. Kenya quickly
grabbed a seat beside Olivia and directed Stephon across from her,
which seated Stephon beside Brian and Nathan on the other end.
Although Kenya noticed the little beads of perspiration on Stephon's
forehead the rest of dinner went quite well. He was able to win the
rest of the family over.

Kenya had been longing for some of Sondra's cooking and Sondra
did not disappoint her. She had the Cornish hen seasoned and ready
along with the brown rice with gravy, spinach casserole and garlic
rolls. The dessert is really what Kenya was waiting for and she would
bake a double chocolate cake for no one but Kenya because no one
else could handle that much chocolate in one bite. Kyla seated in her
high chair between Olivia and Kenya, was delighted as well and also
very hyper as she bared her half toothless smile and rocked from
side to side with her hand clap of approval as Kenya fed the cake to
her. "Thank you Kenya!" Olivia sarcastically exclaimed, laughing as
she ran to catch her daughter while she climbed the furniture after
dinner from the extra caffeine boost." Anytime Olivia! You see, that's
why I'm her favorite Aunty!" "You're her only Aunty!" exclaimed
Olivia as they laughed. Afterwards Stephon followed Nathan and
Brian outside to the back yard patio. Stephon still a little nervous
at the fact that he was meeting Kenya's father, especially with the
intentions that he had for his daughter, but more so of the fact that
Brian was a cop, however he never let it show. Finally Olivia had
alone in Kenya's old room, so with Kyla on her hip, she rushed over
to shut the door so that Sondra wouldn't hear, as she threatened to
have Brian to do a background check on Stephon since Kenya was
too in love to see that regardless of his affluent persona, then for the
first time since Kenya's Freshman year in college Olivia brought up
Dillan Turner, and reminded her that although she was a very smart
girl she could be a little naïve when it came to the opposite sex.

Kenya becoming a little offended started to leave the room, but she'd learned to put her temper in check and realizing that Olivia loved and wanted to protect her, but still dissuaded her from doing the background check and mentioned that she was aware that he didn't have a privileged childhood but neither did they, and probably had to escape the streets in Philadelphia and maybe even embarrassed because of it but he has grown into a very respectable man and has done well for himself, however Olivia was not impressed and even more disappointed in the fact that she had not met any of his family.

As the evening ended Kenya and Stephon made it back to Hartmont. Regardless of Olivia's display of emotions towards Stephon, he'd been having such a good time with Kenya's family that they ended staying longer than expected, so Stephon dropped Kenya off at her house as he walked her in and gave her a big hug and kiss before heading back to his apartment.

# Chapter 12

Stephon was not Myles's main man but by now with the constant phone contact nearly every night seemed to bring them closer, both Myles and Stephon was anxious about getting together, after all it had been 3 months now, so they worked out a plan about what to tell Kenya as Stephon scheduled his days off accordingly. The next day Stephon told Kenya that he'd have an overnight business trip and would have go to Atlanta on Thursday evening so that he could be there early Friday Morning for the meeting. He looked down into her eyes and smiled as they cuddled on the couch in front of the tv. He could see the look of disappointment in her eyes at their first time being apart since they'd been together so he promised that he would make sure he's back on Friday night in time to spend the weekend together. "Maybe you'll run across Myles at the meeting." replied Kenya. "Let's hope not, from what I've heard," replied Stephon as he laughed and tried to keep from showing his nervous sweat at Kenya's mention of Myles's name. Stephon made sure that he returned to town that Friday evening but was completely exhausted. He explained to Kenya that he'd like to just get rested up and they could see one another on Saturday. Not having Stephon around was driving Kenya up the wall. She had become dependent on his companionship like an addiction and had even neglected her best friends Felicia and Tiffany. It would feel a little strange calling either of them now so she did what most people would do when they get bored, and that is turn to social media. The first post she came across was one of her co-worker Terri, who had been unashamedly flirting with Stephon during his visits to the TV Station. Terri posted that she was on a date at a restaurant which happened to be one of Stephon's favorite, then went on to post one of her and Stephon's favorite foods. Could Stephon had really been spending time with Terri? She thought to herself. She didn't want to call him after he told her that he needed the rest, but this was certainly causing her to lose sleep. She stayed up half the night wondering if she had done something to push Stephon away and into Terri's arms, when actually Terri was not the one with whom Stephon was spending time. Terri was merely a pawn that Stephon used in the game he was playing. However there was someone else who had accompanied Stephon on his trip and with whom he was spending time with tonight. Although Terri had been made aware that he and Kenya was not together for the past few days. She also knew his favorite foods and restaurants. He fed Terri information because he knew that she would rub it in Kenya's face the first opportunity she had. Kenya couldn't take it anymore as she sprang out of bed and grabbed her cell phone. She knew better than calling Felicia because she was such a hard sleeper and would not answer her phone, so she dialed Tiffany. "I can't believe you're still up. Don't let Terri do this to you! Don't give her that power because you know she's only posting those things in hopes that you will see it, so that she can have an opportunity to come between you two. Don't give her that chance." After they talked a while as usual she felt much better after speaking with her friend, so she was able to finally fall asleep. The next day Stephon spoke with Myles and he had developed quite an appetite for him and was ready to see him again. He asked that he return and so that he won't make Kenya suspicious to bring her along as well. She would stay at a hotel as he pretended again that he had a business trip. The next morning he called Kenya to apologize and invited her on the next business trip. She was thrilled, so she let Tiffany and Felicia know about their upcoming business trip and decided that she would not give anyone the opportunity to come between her and Stephon as she thought that Terri had, and decided that maybe she needed to step up her game a little. The three went shopping after work for a new outfit for Kenya to wear on the trip along with some sexy lingerie, although Stephon played the perfect gentleman reminding her that though they would be spending the night together on this trip, he would not pressure her for sex. She was done with her shopping and Friday night they were headed back to Atlanta and found a nice restaurant to have a romantic dinner before heading to the room. Settling in for the night they snuggled together kissing and holding one another while they watched TV so that Stephon would be rested up for his early morning meeting. Noticing how quickly he had fallen asleep, she didn't bother to wake him, allowing him to be well rested and was just looking forward to spending time with him on Saturday when the meeting was over. However, the so called meeting, which he spent with Myles in his large and lavish home, lasting well into the afternoon before Stephon was able to take a breather, so that he could call Kenya throughout the day. They talked about their plans for Kenya as well as their plans when Stephon returned to Atlanta as Myles was used to being in control kept suggesting he stay a little longer. Eventually Stephon called to tell her not to wait for him but go ahead and grab a bite to eat before he makes it back to the room because the meeting is lasting way longer than he'd expected and had to supposedly wait for others to arrive.

Stephon awakened to realize that he and Myles had spent the whole day together and it was now nearly 5 o'clock in evening. He quickly jumped out of bed and into the shower, gathering his clothing and grabbing his phone while calling Kenya to let her know that he was on the way. He and Myles exchanged their goodbyes as Myles kidded with him about the way he was running around gathering his things and smiled as he reminded him that the next time he sees him he would be a run-away groom.

Myles took a look at his cell phone to notice that Kenya had attempted to call him earlier in the day since she was in town and had so much spare time. Since she had gotten no answer she had taken a taxi to do a little shopping and decided that she'd have dinner ready in the room when Stephon returned. She'd set the table in the room with a romantic dinner that she'd picked up, along with wine and candles. She'd even laid rose petals up to the tub. He was more than surprised when he stepped into the room to see Kenya in her sexy red lingerie, with rose petals, candle and wine, since he was convinced that she would save herself until their so called wedding night. It was a conversation that they'd had many times. She met him with a long lingering kiss and breast pressed against his chest. This was a different sensation that Stephon was used to. He was much too tired for anything, but the arousal that he was feeling from the warmth and softness of Kenya's body made him a little nervous. He kissed her neck and found himself strangely aroused by the contrast of her soft supple body and the scent of her perfume as he slowly moved his hand over the curves of her body. With his breathing getting heavier he was able to back his way out the door by pretending that he'd had one last minute call to make to finish things up. He called rushed outside and gave Myles a call. "I thought she was going to wait till our so called honeymoon but she wants me tonight!" "It's not like we didn't know that she may eventually expect sex!" he went on to exclaim "besides I don't think I'm able to even keep my eyes open after the day I've had with you." Myles felt a twinge of jealousy wave over him, though he knew that Stephon was going to have to be intimate at some point with Kenya. Ok Stephon. Myles responded out of frustration. "You will need to record everything. I wouldn't want to think that you've enjoyed it." He went on. Stephon returned to the room still surprised at Kenya's aggressiveness as she rubbed her hand over his crotch and they moved to the tub as he undressed and stepped in she gave him a back rub. You feel so tense Kenya replied as she mention that she needed to go reheat the food. As Stephon came out of the bathroom draped in nothing but a robe he hugged her around the waist and thanked her for being so patient with him as they sat down to their romantic meal that she picked out for him. He was barely able to start his meal when Kenya came over to the chair where he was sitting and straddled herself over him. She'd been waiting a long time for this moment although they'd shared plenty of hugs and kisses they'd never taken it to the next level. He embraced her warm soft curves and kissed her taut breast as he reached around her tiny waist to set his phone on the table to record them on the bed, then scooped her up and laid her on the bed in plain view of the camera phone while he kissed repeatedly and traced his tongue down toward the deep intimate parts of her body. She pulled him up as she looked into his eyes then began to kiss her way down his neck then back up, sliding her tongue over his, for a deep and intimate kiss. He could taste the wine on her tongue as he caressed her body and traced his fingers down the arch of her back then over the curve of her hips. His mind began to wonder if she could taste any trace of Myles, or would she notice how inexperienced he was with the female body. Kenya was so enraptured by the male hardness against her thighs. She had very little experience in this area herself and was beginning to wonder if she was moving too fast. Finally his nervousness began get the best of him as well as the exhaustion of the long day that he'd had with Myles, as he exclaimed "Kenya are we going to need to reheat the food again I would hate to see your efforts go to waste but this fine body of yours will not go to waste in anyway, You are so beautiful tonight and I want to savor every moment with you, but I intent to have you for a lifetime, however this food that you have prepared won't last and I am famished. You're gonna need to let me get some strength to handle a woman like you!" Kenya was actually relieved as she was nervous, as she responded "Honey, I know it's been a long day for you and if you'd like we can eat then lay here as long as we're holding one another and just watch a movie in bed." Stephon kissed her and expressed that the meeting was really mentally draining, so he pretended to check his phone one last time so the he could turn the video recorder off. As they finished their meal he held Kenya in his arms apologizing about the evening and intending to watch a movie as he drifted off to sleep no sooner than his head hit the pillow. She wasn't so disappointed because she felt that it would be much more special to save themselves for the honeymoon. They took advantage of the late check out time and had a lazy Sunday morning as they talked and lounged around in bed before getting ready for check out then on to lunch at one of the popular restaurants. They held hands as they shopped afterwards. He bought Kenya a couple of outfits and felt that she deserved them for her patience with him while she stayed in the hotel alone all day plus he felt rejuvenated after being able to get some time in with Myles as they decided on seeing a movie before they heading back home.

# Chapter 13

Stephon was taking full advantages of the privileges he'd been given and worked out his own work schedule since he answered to Myles, and was beginning to live a little too lavish with the credit card as well that Myles had given him. Not wanting to miss out on anything and knowing that there would be no real honeymoon he decided to jump up and go on a mini cruise without advising Myles of what he was doing. He called Kenya up and told her to be ready because he had a surprise for her that would require her to take an extra day off work. Kenya's mind began to wonder what he was up to this time and if he was thinking about eloping as they drove to the port that Friday evening after work, then spent the night in a hotel to leave out early Saturday morning on the cruise. Kenya was wondering where all this extra money was coming from since he should have been saving for the honeymoon. She decided that she would confront him as he pretended to have been given the tickets from one of the stores retailers. She didn't question him any further, but they spent the weekend in style. Kenya called Felicia from the ship to let her know where she was that weekend since they were supposed to have had a movie date that weekend. "I am so jealous!" Felicia shouted over the phone as she laughed. "You guys are always up to something. Have fun and tell us about it on Tuesday!" They spent the day dining and the night dancing and drinking, only coming in the next morning to sleep in. He decided that he would try his hand at some of the subtle flirting with a waitress who went along with his attempts as she bent down low as she served their food as she bare her cleavage as bent down directly in front of Stephon to serve them their food drinks while Stephon laughed to himself as he secretly recorded the waitress with his cell as she took her time cleaning the table next to them and bent over the table wearing her short skirt, as she turned to smile at Myles as she caught a glare from Kenya and decided to straighten her skirt as she walked back into the kitchen. "Are you okay Kenya? "I'm fine Stephon, why do you ask?" Kenya replied pretending as if she had not noticed. "Because you look a little stressed. I brought you on this trip to relax." He watched Kenya's facial expressions as she tried to pretend that everything was just fine. "Sweet heart you know I only have eyes for you." He exclaimed as he kissed her lips and excused himself from the table saying that he had a call from the store as he answered the call from Myles replying to the video he had sent showcasing the flirty waitress and Kenya's facial expressions. He made sure he stood in plain sight of Kenya as he answered his call, so that she would see the waitress circle around him and smile at him as she brushed past. Kenya was on her phone as well sending in a review of the restaurant. Stephon didn't get the reply from Myles that he thought he would with the video. Myles was not at all happy with their week end excursion and let him know that he had been noticing the deficit in his account and he certainly didn't mean for him to spend that amount on Kenya. Myles cut his card off and let him know that he would only allow small increments until he was done with the job of dumping Kenya at the altar. Though his spending had nothing to do with Kenya but was actually looking out for himself and simply bringing Kenya along while given an opportunity. He quickly apologized to Myles for his overspending and agreed that he would curve his spending from now on out. As he went back to the table he was quick to express to Kenya that though his trip was free they would have to budget their spending until the honeymoon. This was the last night of their cruise so they enjoyed their meal and decided to go in a little earlier, Stephon pretending that it was due to the early drive back to Hartmont but in actuality it was because of the fact that he was feeling a little disappointed with the way things had gone with he and Myles during their previous phone conversation and wasn't able to spend Myless money at will as he had done before. Waking up early the next morning, Stephon would normally drive all the way, but agreed to let Kenya drive half way, as he reclined back in the seat, sulking and a little nervous, pretending to have an upset stomach from all the liquor he had consumed the day before.

Although Kenya had been more of the tom boy growing up, she never thought she'd find herself thrilled and elated at the idea of going wedding dress shopping. She let Stephon know that she would need the time to pick out her dress, so the coming weekend will be one for her and the girls to go shopping. As she told Stephon, on the other end of the phone he seemed a little too anxious at the opportunity to finally spend a weekend without Kenya. No sooner than their call ended, he was dialing to make his week end plans, while the opposite was true for Kenya, thrilled at the idea of shopping for her wedding dress, but pouting at the idea of having to be away from Stephon. Regardless, plans were set in motion as she called Olivia to meet them that Saturday morning. Tiffany was raring to go, but unfortunately Felicia wasn't going to make the made the trip with them that weekend because of a last minute assignment that she said she needed to be working on. Kenya expressed her disappointment but didn't let that ruin her trip with Olivia and Tiffany, as they excitedly made their plans to head out to Atlanta for Saturday morning, where they would be spending the night. They made it into Atlanta by lunch time as their bags were being unloaded at the Hotel Kenya decided to give Stephon a short call let him know that they had arrived at the hotel, unable to reach him, she left him a voice mail as they started their dress hunt. Kenya knew exactly the first store that she would like to stop and was usually very decisive but it seemed that she had taken on Olivia's personality as a diva when it came to shopping, trying on nearly every dress in the shop. It was the same at the next shop. She tried on a few and Olivia being brutally honest let her know how she looked in the dresses. Finally there was a shop that they had come to where there was a dress that all three was able to agree upon, so they texted a picture to Felicia and Sondra. They all agreed that Kenya was beautiful in the one that she had chosen. When she got to the register and she was told the price she exclaimed, "There is no wonder it's so beautiful!" She had been told by Sondra to call Nathan when she was ready to purchase because he wanted to pay for it and wouldn't have it any other way, so they gave him a call as he at the price but was honored to purchase his daughter's wedding dress as he spoke with the sales attendant over the phone. It was truly beautiful with its intricate white lace and sequin top with full length lace sleeves and its long satin train. They'd picked the perfect vale to go with it. Kenya would be beautiful. The colors that she had chosen for her wedding was quite different that Olivia's and she intended it that way. Her bridemaids dresses had already been ordered and they were periwinkle blue and ivory, and was able to find the perfect venue for such short notice. The wedding would be in Cantonville and held outdoors on the patio of the Cantonville Recreation Center which happened to overlook Cantonville Lake. Of course Stephon had talked the station manager into having it televised live for her friends and fans in Hartmont. Excited about finding a dress they decided to have dinner at the hotel that they were staying in, since Kenya was driving and wanted to be able to have a drink to celebrate. As they waited on their food, Olivia called again to check on Kyla for what seemed like the hundredth time since this was the first time that she had spent the night without her, but she was sure that Brian was doing a good job. Brian was working the night shift so he'd dropped Kyla off to spend the night with Sondra and Nathan, who were thrilled to keep her. As Kenya began to talk about Stephon Tiffany made mention of Terri but Kenya quickly averted the subject, however not before Olivia zoned in judging by the look on her face, particularly since she was still being skeptical of Stephon, but she didn't feel that this was a time or place to make an issue of it. Of course Kenya painted a picture that made him look like an angel, which is exactly how she saw him. As Olivia excused herself to step into the restroom Kenya quietly warned Tiffany not to mention those things that were going on with those women at the office. By the time they made it back to the room which they shared with double beds and adjoining suites Kenya gave Stephon a call to let him know how her day had gone. Although the three were exhausted, they stayed up half the night talking and laughing. They were up early because Olivia had awakened them because she was missing her darling dumpling as she called her and her hubby, so they got dressed and after having breakfast headed back to Hartmont. Kenya and Tiffany gave Olivia a hug as she hopped in her car and took off for Cantonville. Olivia didn't meet Felicia this trip, so she told Kenya to let her know that she was sorry she missed her and wasn't going to hang around to see Stephon, but wasn't that enthused about seeing Stephon anyhow. This happened to be his weekend to work, so Kenya had plenty to do around the house before she saw him that evening. He gave her a big hug and kiss when she answered the door. Although his weekend was rather preoccupied, he actually felt himself missing Kenya, and was glad to see her face.

# Chapter 14

Myles, out of his control and a slight twinge of jealousy coming on, was ready for the plans to progress. Stephon reminded him that he had no feelings for Kenya. His love of money overpowered anything that he feel for anyone. Myles was convinced that Kenya was having it too good off of his money and wanting to see her suffer, urged Stephon to get her fired, so the next day Stephon was at the station during lunch break making sure that as Kenya was going on the air she'd spotted something that seemed more that just friendly between Stephon and Terri. She thought she noticed as Terri whispered something into Stephon's ear that she reached her hand assumedly across his crotch. Terri was turned out to be the perfect pawn to play on Kenya's mind, and the mind games had definitely began to intensify. Terri was well known to be a flirt. Because of that Kenya requested that he not exchange phone numbers with her, but she could have sworn that she saw them exchange phone numbers. Kenya's inability to concentrate did not go unnoticed by the station manager, who had been picking up on the fact that Kenya's quality of work had begun to diminish quite a bit lately. She could not gather herself the whole show as she watched Terri throw a fake smile in her direction as Stephon left the studio having return to work himself. Kenya gave Stephon a call after work. He let her know that he was still a little tired from the weekend so he'd see her on Tuesday, which she also felt was a little strange since normally they would just watch TV together when he was tired, she was beginning to have second thoughts but she had already put a lot of time and money into the wedding and thought maybe it was just her. Bored because once again, Felicia was out assignment and Tiffany busy with her own chores at home. Olivia grading papers, so Kenya turned again to social media as a cure for her boredom and the first posts she notices is Terri's about how she is on a dinner date with an attractive gentleman and it happened to be Stephon's favorite restaurant. She dismisses any thoughts of infidelity of her new fiancé and busied herself with chores till bedtime. When she called Stephon that night the call went straight to voicemail. She seemed bothered the next day as Terri passes by and mentioned in Kenya hearing about how she didn't know how she would make it through the day because her date had kept her up last night. When she finally heard from Stephon she mentioned to him what she thought she'd seen the day before. He laughed and told her that she had a little jealous bone. He mentioned to her that he is just a personable guy and laughs and talks with everyone. For the first time she felt a little anger towards Stephon's insensitivity, as he asked if she felt that they may need to delay the wedding. After putting so much into it and not wanting to deal with the embarrassment after he'd pressed to be so public she let him know that she was fine and would go on with the plans that they have made, just as Stephon knew she would. "Good sweetheart because I don't think that I could live without you in my life any longer. I can't wait for you to be my wife. Even if you are a little jealous" he laughed.

Some of the other ladies who were friends with Terri whispered and stared as she passed by the next day. She had just been called away on special assignment as Stephon showed up and Terri was the first to greet him as he seemed mesmerized by Terri as she walked past then looking up to wave at Kenya, making sure she sees him as looks at Terri as though he had ex-ray vision as she walked past and they exchanged words, but it was Felicia who walks up to Stephon to exchange words and distracts Terri's sexy glare. Kenya was relieved as she thought to herself, Felicia to the rescue, and motioned to them that she would call later as she was whisked out the back door by the camera crew. Though Kenya was leaving Stephon seemed to be lingering around with some of her co-workers with whom he worked out with giving them work out tips. Kenya was usually very confident and not a jealous person but she could not help but to feel some jealousy and was totally distracted during the assignment. Stephon had expressed to Myles that he would love to see the two fight over him, and looks like he might just get what he wanted, as Kenya went on air she stuttered and mispronounced words all evening it was Terri who was there waiting to point it out. There was no way Kenya could take what Terri was saying as constructive after all she'd seen earlier that caused her to be so distracted, as Kenya became defensive and loud with her everyone seemed to stop and stare but before Kenya could finish her sentence she the secretary interrupted to let her know that she had received an emergency phone call. As she went into her office to take the call it was Sondra letting her know that she had been trying to reach her and she realized that she still had her phone on silent, Sondra went on to let her know that her Nathan had been admitted into the hospital, all Kenya could say was "I'm on my way Mama!" as she ran to let her Station Manager know what had happened, the Station Manager also let her know that there was something that she needed like to talk to her about when she returned. But Kenya couldn't think of anything right now, all she could do was get home, pack a few bags and get to Cantonville to check on Nathan. When she got there, she was told that he had suffered a light heart attack but everything would be fine. He would just spend a few days there in the hospital. Later that night she returned Stephon's calls and let him know what had happened. He expressed to her that he was very worried about her, especially when she wasn't at work or at home. She spent the next few days there until Nathan was ready to come home and Stephon came down to visit on the last day when he was released. With he and Olivia still not feeling one another, Kenya decided not to tell her about her feelings and those things that had gone on at the job. Their main focus was on Nathan.

# Chapter 15

When she returned to work there was a note on her desk to see the Station Manager. She arrived in Mrs. Stanfield's office and she expected that she would be warned regarding her work performance but didn't expect to hear the news that Mrs. Stanfield had for her. As she sat there she was hearing the words that she was having to let her go. She mentioned her work performance, the tension between she and other office staff and the time she has had to take off the job has caused him to have to release her. Kenya walked out of the office head spinning from the news that she'd just heard. Co-workers asked if she was okay as she walked slowly to the hall, apparently she was crying without even realizing it till the teardrop roll down her cheek onto her blouse. She grabbed her purse and heading out the door as Tiffany and Felicia packed her things for her and brought them to her home. When she called Stephon he played the role of the supportive fiancé and told her he would be there for her no matter what and the wedding, only a month away, would go on and nothing was stopping them. He made her feel that he was invincible and would always be there. When Stephon called Myles to tell him the news he was beaming as a man with his first child. Myles mentioned things were going better than had expected. That next day Stephon invited her to his work place for lunch. She had been a well-known personality in the city and Stephon had told his co-workers about her dismissal. This is something she would rather not broadcast, and found herself embarrassed as she walked through the store but regardless he introduced her around as if he was proud of her. Some whispered and glared, but there were some who were very supportive. He met Kenya at home that night and even offered to let her move into his apartment with him, but she let him know that her savings was enough to hold her over for a while until she found something else. He went on to mention that they would be married soon and had no need for two places. After all, Myles would be thrilled to see her sell her home and belongings to be not only jobless but homeless as well.

As she left Stephon's and settled in for bed her restlessness gave way to sleep but the stress of her father's heart attack and losing her job was enough to re-trigger the nightmares of Chloe. This time was so much clearer that she could almost understand what Chloe was saying but not quite as Chloe moved closer Kenya began to kick the covers off and wake up gasping for breath. She was wet with sweat as if she'd actually been under water. Kenya was never a cry baby but since she met Stephon she realized that she has been very emotional, and all she could do was cry tonight. She didn't want to wake Stephon but she called him, and he again playing the concerned fiancé came over to check on her. Since it was 11pm instead of driving back home, he brought clothes to wear to work, so that he'd spend the night with Kenya. As he listened to Kenya talk about her night mare and her childhood with her friend Chloe, which he'd heard before but Myles's version, he did not expect what happened next. As she talked about Myles and how she loved that family, Stephon began to feel a little too much for her and didn't feel that she deserved what was happening to her but with the mission that he had to accomplish so he tried to shake it off however as she began to talk about her father and losing her job at this time in her life he felt himself reaching out to hug her, she mentioned Myless family and how she loved them and he couldn't understand how Myles could feel the way he did about Kenya. As he listened to her, he embraced her they began to kiss, realizing he was beginning to care a little too much but could not pull himself away this time. He found that he didn't want to pull away as he massaged her tense body and held close. He did not resist the urge to sink into the warmth and softness of her caress. His mind now both blown by his desire and tortured by his feelings for her as he held her close and lay staring into her angelic face as she slept and wondered how Myles could hate her so much over something that happened when they were only children and had no control over and wondered as well how a man so perfect and flawless as Myles, one who had the persona of a doctor or a politician and seemed to have it all together be so out of control. He realized the fact that he had always been so busy controlling everything with all of his money and power that to be out of control was driving him mad and realized that with Myles it was really driven by envy and control. Kenya was the one person that he has not been able to destroy no matter what he did to control the outcome she would always overcome and he would literally go crazy if he knew that he had not just had sex with Kenya but had made love to Kenya last night and passionately savored every moment of it. Kenya was so resilient and Myles was becoming obsessed with trying to control something that he had no control over. That night was something that he could not let Myles find out, however, Myles noticed that Stephon did not return his call the next morning. He brought Kenya breakfast in bed before he showered as he got ready for work as she fell harder for him and he was falling for her, confused by his own feelings and sexuality, as he kissed her with a deeper passion and stared into her eyes a little longer before heading out the door on the way to work. He found himself perplexed, knowing that it would be definitely devastating to Kenya for him to leave her at this point. As he thought about all the things that Kenya had gone through because of his part in this deception, along with all the wonderful things that she had said about Myles and his family it made him more sympathetic towards Kenya as he thought about her throughout his day at work.

Stephon rang the doorbell as he stepped inside surprising Kenya with a box of pizza, as she kissed him on the lips "You're just in time because I was trying to figure what to cook for dinner." Kenya expressed as she took out a bottle of red wine and they sat on the floor in front of the television. He stared at her, taking notice of her every move, as she paused to ask what he was looking at. He began to notice that this laugh of hers was no longer annoying but very contagious, it made him laugh and all he wanted to do was make her happy. Looking into her eyes all he wanted to do was protect her as he smiled at her quirkiness while they playfully wrestled on the carpet. The sound of the rain made the atmosphere even more romantic as they drifted off to sleep while they lay there on the soft carpet with her head against his chest. It wasn't the sound of the rain, but the sound of his heartbeat that she was listening to as she drifted off, and it was her face that he saw as he closed his eyes and dozed in his comfortable position. About an hour had passed when he awakened and nudged at her then helped her into the bedroom, and into the bed since she was already wearing pajamas, as she looked up into his face, then rolled over and went right back to sleep. He pulled the covers over her shoulders while she reached for his hand but he had to get all the lights turned off and get back to his place since the next day was a work day for him. He made sure the doors were locked as he headed out to his car.

Briefly checking his cell phone as he pulled into the parking lot of his apartment complex he noticed that he had missed a couple of calls from Myles but didn't bother to call back, as he headed inside and got himself ready for bed and for the next day, not just for work, but for what he would say to Myles. The next morning as he got dressed for work, he pulled out his business suit for the day and thought back on the night before, having to shake it off because he had to be business as usual if he wanted to get paid, as he picked up his cell phone to dial Myles while coming up with an excuse as to the reason that he didn't return his calls as he hopped into his black mercedes and headed off for his work day, but that didn't stop Myles from feeling a little restless at Stephon's ignoring him. He's been doing that quite a bit lately, Myles thought to himself as he looked over his calendar to plan a time to pay a little visit to Hartmont.

Now it was Myles having a hard time focusing and concentrating realizing that Stephon seemed to grow a little too soft with his emotions toward Kenya and had the feeling that more had happened between the two than he was willing to tell and he began to hate Kenya even more. With all his money and all his power he was still not able to control Kenya. He began asking Stephon to dump her before the wedding and move back to Atlanta. Stephon agreed but Myles noticed that he had begun to procrastinate and come up with excuses so Myles was growing more and more frustrated with the situation. He hated feeling out of control and was beginning to hate Kenya more and more as the days went by. They were now less than a month away from the wedding date with arrangements made and caterers hired.

# Chapter 16

The wedding date grew closer and Myles more restless. He couldn't stand it anymore, nervous that Stephon just may change his mind about backing out of this wedding he refused to lose one more thing to Kenya. Making last minute choices Kenya flipped hastily through a catalog of arrangements for the reception but losing patience she hopped in her car and drove to Stephon's apartment for his advice on the décor with Myles following from a distance and watching their interaction as Stephon seemed a little startled met her at the door and played it off by giving her a big kiss as he ran to the laundry room to get a basket of clothes that were drying. Not expecting her he had left his phone on the table, something he'd never done but being thrown off guard this time he left his phone where Kenya could see it. She'd never thought anything of it so when Myles called Stephon's phone to let him know that he was in town Kenya picked it up to take it to him. She would have never known that it was Myles calling because he would never list Myles's name on the phone in case she did see it but as Kenya picked up Stephon's phone to take it to him she did noticed that he was in the middle of a sexually explicit text in which the person was asking when they would get together again. Looking closer she noticed the name that accompanied that message was not familiar as she nervously scrolled through the messages before he could return into the room and came across a nude photo. She realized that the name was an alias as her heart skipped a beat.

Hurt to the core, she wondered how he could have been betraying her this way. Never suspecting in a million years that this to be was having an affair and particularly not with this person. She could not believe her eyes, bursting into tears and a heart aching sob as she threw the phone across the room without confronting him she ran out of the apartment before Stephon could return. If he'd ever wanted to destroy Kenya this was the perfect way to do it. Myles sitting in the car from a distance and seeing her rush from the apartment sought opportunity to follow after, deciding that he would not need to let Stephon know that he was in town as he set his phone to the side watching her leave Stephon's apartment alone and distraught then taking off like a bat out of hell as she sped along the highway. She quickly pulled into the driveway then ran into the house slamming the door shut as emotions ran through her mind. Unable breath and feeling as if she was having a panic attack. Angry and hurt and just wanting something to dull the pain she reached for a bottle of wine that she kept stored away.

Myles gave her time to enter into the house and sulk for a while before he came to the door. She was just about to give Tiffany a call as the doorbell rang. She quickly opened the door assuming that it was Stephon following after her but was both surprised and relieved to see Myles standing there, assuming that maybe he was stopping by on his way to Cantonville to see her father after his heart attack she invited him in and offered him a drink. As she began to ramble on trying to explain her tear streaked face and going on and on about Stephon and what she had just come to find Myles stared at her with his hidden rage until he could no longer take it, she thinking that his stare was a look of disgust about what her fiancé had just done to her, but he could care less about Stephon's other lover and how she was feeling. Consumed with his hatred for her, with fists clinched, he snapped, throwing his drink against the wall as he pulled out a gun and snatched Kenya by the hair as she screamed and stared into his face in disbelief. She couldn't put together what was happening. She found herself screaming but her screams go unheard by the neighbors since their houses were so spread apart. As he clinched her hair in his hands, she swung at him she was astounded at his strength as he grabbed her hands and held both of her hands together with one hand as if she was a little child and the gun in the other. "Do you think that Stephon cares anything for you?" snarled Myles pulling her face around so that he could see look on her face when he tells her that he and Stephon are lovers. How could she bear this, with all that she has gone through. This is unbelievable. She wondered if she were dreaming. This man, whom she thought of as a big brother along with the man with whom she had just spent each and every day with for the past six months, who'd swept her off her feet. The man with whom she is supposed to be marrying in only a few days. She had so many emotions going through her head. As he again grabbed and held her hands together with one hand and a gun in the other, he placed his gun on the table as she struggled to get to it. He grabbed some rope then tape from underneath his jacket as Kenya screamed for help. This explains why he showed up wearing a jacket in the summer time as she noticed, but she was too frantic about her own situation to dwell on that. Never would she have figured that Myles was coming to hurt her. She tried to fight him but to no avail as he nearly knocked her unconscious with a blow to the back of the head with his revolver then tying her up and gagging her mouth before carrying her out to the car as if she was a ragged doll and throwing her into the back seat as he slammed the car door and ran back to close her front door so that it would not alert the neighbors if they happened to pass by. He hopped into the car looking at her through his rear view mirror as he sped off, expressing to her all the sorted details of the past few six months. He even told her that he was behind her break up with Dillan, as well as her firings. She could not believe her ears when he let her listen to some of the intimate phone calls and conversations that she and Stephon shared as she lay on the back seat drifting in and out of consciousness due to the blow to the back of the head from Myless gun. She dreamed of Chloe each time and would wake herself up. This time her dreams were more vivid than ever, as she found herself drifting towards Chloe floating lifelessly in the mirky water until she was right upon her, then as always, her eyes suddenly came open and she became animated in the water as she reached forward and stared with those oddly colored but beautiful eyes. Her clothes flowed about in the water as she brought her attention to a pendant that she wore about her neck. For the first time she was able to hear at least some of the things that Chloe was saying. She made mention of the resillant and motioned in the water as the pendant that that she was wearing floated about her neck. Kenya recognized the pendant and began to remember the day that her Grandma Rose had given it to her. In this dream Chloe went on to tell her to save her brother. "What do you mean save your brother!" she started to become breathless as she went on "Your brother is trying to kill me!" she came to as she attempted to scream, gasping for air but her mouth was gagged as she looked up to notice Myles staring at her through the rear view mirror as she lay bound on the back seat. About an hour out she noticed the tops of the trees and realized that they were going back to Cantonville. Kenya was able to spit the gag out of her mouth to be able to ask him why he was doing this. Myles let her know that all he has done he has done for his little sister. He replied "She never had the chance to graduate, date, have a husband or children, but looks like you won't have that chance either!" He looks at her with rage in his eyes as he pulled to a screeching halt then jumped out of the car and approaching her door. He pulled her out of the car as he gagged her mouth once again as she realized that they were back at the Cantonville Lake where Chloe drowned. Was she about to die only a block away from home as she longed to see her Parents one last time. If only Daddy could hear my screams she thought to herself. Myles knew that at this hour there would be no one there to see them at the area of the lake nearest the woods, in that secluded area where they'd all gather to play as kids. Kenya terrified at what was going on attempted to scream through the gag as he forced her down to the banks of the Cantonville Lake. She shuffled along with ankles loosely bound, again trying to fight him as he knocked her into the water hands bound, then jerked her back up. They both stopped in their tracks as they notice the shadow of a figure appear although they heard no one. Myles dropped his gun to his side, not believing what he was seeing, beginning to think that his mind was playing tricks on him. Kenya had gotten her hands free and reached for the gun as he composed himself and held it to Kenya's head. Kenya was relieved that someone had shown up in the knick of time, but attempted to scream all the more when she turned to realize who it was, that the figure that appeared was little Chloe. The same little Chloe with those long ponytails and beautiful strange eyes. It as if it were yesterday. This time she looked her directly into her eyes as if she were looking through her. Kenya became calm realizing that Chloe was not there to hurt her as she pleaded with Myles not to harm her because Kenya is her friend. She told him how Kenya and Olivia tried to save her, but she was carried away because it was just her time to go. She turned and smiled at Kenya and said "I told you in your dreams that it wasn't your fault and that I'd be back to visit you again one day." Kenya began to cry. Myles broke down into tears as he told Chloe how much he loved and missed her and wished that he had never let her leave his room that day. He tried reaching out his hand to touch her as if he'd keep her there but she was translucent, as she told him she loved him too. Kenya tried to reach for Myles's gun again while he was distracted but he turned and slapped her across the face as snapped back into his own reality as he told Chloe that he can never forgive the Palmer's for what they let happen to her and that Kenya was living the life that she should have been living. With a look of disappointment and sadness, Chloe faded away. Turning to Kenya with eyes full of tears and rage, "Once again I've lost my sister, and it is all your fault" Myles shouted as he held the gun to Kenya's head. "I didn't want to kill you Kenya, I just wanted to watch you suffer, but I can't allow you to take away anything else that I love. I won't let that happen anymore. I'm going to have to put an end to this, it's just too much!" Kenya looked him in the eyes as she tried pleading with him through her muffled mouth piece. She saw the look that he had in his eyes was such hatred, at the same time she saw hopelessness and sadness and her heart broke for Myles as she tried reasoning with herself as to how she could be having these feelings toward him while he held a gun to her head and about to take her life. As she saw the look of determination in his eyes she gave up any attempts to scream and just whispered a little prayer as she shut her eyes and waited for the bullet to pierce her skull and end her life. She could hear the sound of a bullet as her body became numb. She held on to Myles as they sank into the water which seemed to be turning into blood. As she was beginning to choke she could see Chloe. This time Kenya wasn't afraid. Reaching out for Chloe's hand she closed her eyes as the water began to fill her lungs, then waited for the next moment of her eternity as she felt herself rising. Stephon quickly pumped Kenya's chest and cleared her airway as she coughed up the water that filled her lungs. He then rushed back to Myles as he begged and pleaded with him to live as the blood poured out of his chest. She could hear sirens in the back ground as she lay there while Stephon told Myles he loved him and he didn't want to shoot him, but he just couldn't let him kill Kenya behind an accident that happened as tragic as it was when they were only kids. In all the commotion that was going on as she lay on the banks of the Cantonville Lake she noticed something in the bushes and as she reached over to pick it up she noticed that it was the pendant necklace that Chloe was wearing. She held it close to her heart and tucked away in her wet bosom as she thought back on the day at the day the Grandma Rose had given it to her, Chloe had fallen in their yard and scraped her knee while they were outside playing. Grandma Rose came over to her as she was about to cry, taking the necklace from around her own neck and placing it around Chloe's, as she told her she had to be tough like her mother Val, then went on sometimes seeming to make up her on words and language. The girls looked at Grandma Rose, as Kenya whispered to Chloe, "Why is she calling that pendant she gave you a, as she paused, a resillant?" "No, not the pendant, but the person wearing it" Val chuckled as she stood watching from the doorway. "She is speaking of "the resilient," those who fall or get knocked down and right up, dust themselves off and keep on going even stronger!" They began to stare at Val with that same look of bewilderment. "Just take care of the pendant that Grandma gave you, you'll understand when you're older" exclaimed Val as she looked at Chloe while she got her scrape cleaned up and put the bandage her knee, patted on her on her behind sending us back to play as Chloe tucked the pendant underneath her t-shirt. Kenya turned to look at Grandma Rose as they headed back out to play as Grandma Rose repeated that strange word "resillant" while this time pointing at Kenya. The girls later made light of it yet in the back of her mind Kenya was honored that she would point her out and hoped that she was as Grandma Rose had said. Unfortunately it didn't seem as though Myles was going to bounce back as he lay on the embankment with the gunshot wound to his chest. Kenya crawled over beside him not knowing what to say or do, she showed him the pendant that she had in her hand. As his eyes locked onto it there was a look of recognition and whatever sentimental value this pendant held it seemed to change his whole demeanor as his features softened and he looked into Kenya's eyes "What have I done" he mumbled regretfully as he winced in pain. The pendant seemed to serve as proof that he was not delusional when he saw Chloe earlier and neither had she been lost to him forever. Kenya calmed him as she held his hand and asked if he would forgive her for Chloe's sake as he stared at Kenya with his breathing becoming more labored then finally shook his head yes as if the tears that he held in during that day at the funeral began to flow freely. He asked Kenya and Stephon if they would forgive him for all the trouble he had caused them both as they kneeled beside him, one on side and one on the other, as Kenya who never saw herself as a deeply religious person began to lead them in a prayer that seemed to give him an unexplainable peace. She looked up and through the gathering crowd as if she were to see Chloe. Stephon held onto Myles's hand as his breathing became more labored. "I'm so sorry but I had to stop you!" Stephon sobbed uncontrollably as Myles breathed his last breath. Once again an all too familiar scene at Cantonville Lake for the Vincents, as the Paramedics, this time along with Police show up, first on the scene was Kenya's brother in law Brian who had heard on the scanner what was going on as he rushed to Kenya's side. Mr. and Mrs. Vincent had arrived at Myles's side as Kenya was taken away on a stretcher. She attempted to describe to police what had gone on that night, but had to catch herself as she went on knowing the mention of Chloe would be unbelievable, so she kept it to herself. The Palmer's had made it to the lake hugging and holding onto Kenya as they loaded her onto the ambulance, as they looked around to see the Vincent family. After the all the family that had gathered left the Hospital, Olivia spent the night there with Kenya instead of resting Kenya giving Olivia the details of what had gone on, Olivia letting her know that she'd had an uneasy feeling about Stephon but had never suspected Myles in all those years. Kenya realized she was still holding the pendant in hand that she found at the lake, waving it before Olivia's face mid-sentence to show it to her. Do you remember this Olivia? Kenya interrupted. "Yes, I remember that pendant. That's the pendant that Chloe used to wear." Olivia exclaimed. Kenya's eyes filling with tears "I have so much more to tell you" exclaimed Kenya with her voice trailing off finally drifting into sleep from the effects of the meds. Olivia stared at her sister's now calm childlike features as she drifted away, settling onto the couch beside her bed as she stared in bewilderment at the pendant that Kenya lay clutching in her hand. Kenya drifting off into sleep looking forward to seeing her little friend in her dreams, but Chloe wasn't there this time regardless she knew that they all, Chloe, Myles and Grandma Rose were at peace now.

# Chapter 17

The next day Kenya was released from the hospital and no sooner than Olivia drove her home to their Parents house, and everyone making sure she was comfortable in bed, than she was watching through the window to make sure that Olivia had driven away, then went to grab the keys from the kitchen counter hopped into Sondra's car managing to avoid their attention and was on her way to the police station, making it there just as Stephon was being released. So many questions running through her mind for Stephon, as she abruptly approached him as he was exiting the lobby. He came to a halt staring intently and passionately at Kenya as she blurted out "How did you know where we were Stephon?" Careful to answer every question as he explained thank God that through everything that was happening she still had her phone in her. "Yes" she responded, "I had placed it in my pant pocket when I answered the door, but it was so frustrating because my hands were tied I couldn't get to my phone." "I had a tracker placed on your phone so that I could keep up with your where abouts" Stephon went on. He mentioned that the last night he had gotten too distracted and didn't realize she was coming over when she did. "Yes I found out just how distracted you were when I read the text that you had going on with Jeff" responded Kenya. "I still can't believe that everything was just a lie! Why Stephon, would you go through such lengths to hurt me?" Kenya expressed with tears beginning to well in her eyes as she stared intently into his.

"Money and greed Kenya" he answered ashamedly, looking away for a moment, then back into Kenya's eyes, "that's the thing that has motivated me all my life." He put his hands to together as he went on "I had no idea that things would go this far! With Myles being so used to controlling everything and everyone he became obsessed when he could not control you. Everything that he threw at you, you were able to overcome, and when I started to have feelings for you he became so angry and was even more intent on destroying you, to the point that he couldn't even control himself" explained Stephon. Kenya sighed as she let him know that she'd never forget all those things that he'd done, but she would also will also always be thankful for the fact that he saved her life. Stephon still apologizing but realizing that he can never apologize enough for all else he'd done. He let her know as well what a good friend she had in Tiffany and particularly in Felicia as he let her know that Felicia had confronted him at the Station on the night that she had left on assignment to let him know that she did not trust him and would have him investigated, so they threatened each other. "I had her number blocked from your phone and she was probably convinced that I had told you about her confrontation and that you were angry with her. I am so sorry but I knew that she would ruin things." She looked at him with disgust and just as that root of bitterness was taking hold, he went on to say, "I called her when I was on the way here and told her that it was I who had her number blocked". "I'm pretty sure she has been trying to reach you so please give her a call when you get a new phone and your numbers established to let her know that you are okay." He looked deep into her eyes as he went on to say "Kenya you have such a good heart, and will make some man a good wife and be a wonderful mother one day. He will be a very lucky man and trust me I know." "No Stephon, he is going to be a blessed man" Kenya smiled as she responded, noticing that finally he felt more free to express himself. She managed to give him a hug and wave him on to the awaiting vehicle in the distance as Jeff Williams from Stroudman and Marcus was there to pick him up and moving back to Atlanta with him. Stephon turn to wave one last time, as he looked from the distance and would like to have turned back to give her another hug, but didn't feel as though he deserved it as he turned to get into the vehicle while still looking back at her. Kenya's heart seemed to brake all over again with the finality of it all as she watched them drive out of view. Her life had been an endless whirlwind and there was a long road ahead, but she was just thankful for her life. The tears began to roll down her face as she walked back to the car reflecting back over the last six months of her life. A reality of loneliness hit her but she shook it off and thought of how she would rebuild her career. She said a silent prayer and there was that calm once again, a consolation and an unexplainable peace that would encompass and fill what would seemed to be the loneliest moment of her life. She knew she had family on her side and wasn't completely alone, as did the Vincent family.

As Kenya sat there on her bed looking like a little girl again just reflecting over all that had gone on in her life, eyes fixed on the pendant and in her thoughts as she reclined back on her pillow as she held it up before her face suddenly she grabbed her phone that had finally come in the mail and started making that calls to cancel wedding plans but instead following her whimsical mind, gave the Vincent's a call. She was able to convince them to use the Cantonville Recreation Center for Myles's a dinner in tribute of Myles, following the funeral since it had already been booked and paid for and was something she wanted to do for them. After all the trouble that he'd put Kenya through, they were hesitant but reluctantly agreed since she persisted, so complete with flowers in periwinkle blue and ivory with silver ribbons, food and caterers in place the Cantonville Recreation Center seemed oddly perfect, as they transformed it into a celebration of life and could not have been more befitting for someone who loved his family so passionately and symbolic of the peace he'd finally found. As the evening came to an end Olivia couldn't help but notice her brother in law Teddy as he stood there regarding Kenya from a distance, hands in pockets as he stood, after all these years still mesmerized. Olivia quietly snickered remembering their days as the neighborhood kids in the backyard of the Palmer house she gently gave Brian's shirt a tug, pointing at Teddy, as he pondered whether to approach Kenya as she stood there. He finally gained the courage to approach her, walking up behind her and placing his jacket over her shoulders as she stood overlooking the water, no words spoken but his presence and a comforting smile, as the families gathered in all their resilience, in that gathering spot overlooking Cantonville Lake.

CPSIA information can be obtained
at www.ICGtesting.com
Printed in the USA
BVHW071704020119
536873BV00006B/613/P